A
CROW
TO PLUCK

VENGEANCE... AT ANY PRICE

A CROW

TO PLUCK

VENGEANCE... AT ANY PRICE

BOB GIEL

GALWAY
PRESS

an imprint of

OGHMA CREATIVE MEDIA

OGHMA

CREATIVE MEDIA

Galway Press
An imprint of Oghma Creative Media, Inc.
2401 Beth Lane, Bentonville, Arkansas 72712

Library of Congress Cataloging-in-Publication Data

Names: Giel, Bob, author.
Title: A Crow to Pluck/Bob Giel.
Description: First Edition. | Bentonville: Galway, 2019.
Identifiers: LCCN: 2018944176 | ISBN: 978-1-63373-435-7 (hardcover) |
ISBN: 978-1-63373-436-4 (mass media paperback) |
ISBN: 978-1-63373-437-1 (eBook)
Subjects: | BISAC: FICTION/Westerns |
FICTION/Action & Adventure | FICTION/Historical
LC record available at: https://lccn.loc.gov/2018944176

Galway Press mass media paperback edition February, 2019

Cover & Interior Design by Casey W. Cowan
Editing by Dennis Doty

This work would not have been possible without the support and assistance of my family. They have always been my rock through the good and bad times, cheering me on when hope was thin and ragged.

ACKNOWLEDGEMENTS

To GIVE THE READER A BIT of insight into how I shape my characters, let me explain that I use actors with whom I'm familiar to allow me to envision their physical characteristics, mannerisms, way of speaking, etc. So, right off the bat, I must acknowledge the contribution of Randolph Scott. Mr. Scott passed away long before the concept of this book awakened me at two in the morning, screaming, "Write me! Write me!" However, his body of work stands as an example of the stoic man of the frontier that Cope Worley represents to me. Immediately after the first scream, the second cried, "Randolph Scott!" That told me how to proceed.

Deep appreciation goes to the Western Writers of America, whose annual convention gave me the venue with which to present my work to several publishers' representatives in attendance. WWA's support has been invaluable to me.

Equal gratitude is due Oghma Creative Media, the principals of which saw in my work something worth publishing. Casey Cowan and Venessa Cerasale were receptive, encouraging and supportive of an unknown author in whom they saw potential.

Last, but certainly not least, the contributions of my editor, Dennis Doty, to the integrity and accuracy of this novel have served to make it better every step of the way. His devotion to the written word and his vast knowledge of the history of the West and the world of the Western never ceases to amaze me.

I have been truly blessed in this venture, from start to finish. My gratitude is boundless.

COPE

AND

E.J.

1

THAT BULLET'S GOT TO COME OUT!"

The words seemed distant, and Cope guessed it was the voice of the doctor. Everything appeared cloudy. Vaguely, he remembered being shot. Pain, a lot of pain. It's in my shoulder, he thought. Dizzy. Something stroked his head. Trying to focus on the figure above him proved futile, but he was able to identify it when the voice said, "Do whatever you have to." E.J. was here with him, wherever here was. Home? The doctor's office? Too fuzzy to tell, but it was all right, as long as E.J. stayed with him.

He assumed time had passed but he could not be sure. Something pressed on his forehead. Maybe E.J. kissed him. Nothing was certain. Someone lifted his head and placed something against his lips. A glass maybe? Maybe water. The liquid crossed his lips into his mouth. Not water. Way too bitter. Laudanum maybe. He swallowed hard. More came, and he swallowed that as well. Yeah, laudanum. Had that before. Bad stuff—Dizziness getting worse—Getting dark now—Can't—

PAIN—OH, GOD, IT HURTS—DIGGING, biting, probing, pulling, *tearing....*

"Got it!"

Oh. Little better now. Getting dark again....

———

RUNNING, CHASING THAT KID. CAN'T CATCH up to him. What was that behind him? A bullet? Chasing him? Got to avoid it! Got to duck it!

Awakening with a start that jolted his body and made him explicitly aware of the pain in his chest, he struggled, in the half-conscious world he found himself re-entering, not to return to the dreaming. His vision cloudy, his head still spinning, he tried to focus on the where and when, then on the here and now. None of it worked. He remembered the chase and the search and that idiot firing on him. Must have been hit, he thought. The pain was evidence of that. He fired as the kid ran, didn't he? He thought so, but still unclear, uncertain.

Blinking his eyes caused the scene in front of him to clear a little. Fuzzy around the edges but, yeah, it was home. The bedroom. In bed. E.J.—where was she?

"E.J.!"

He found his voice, what there was of it, rough, scratchy and weak. Mouth too dry. Felt like cotton. He tried again, a little stronger this time.

"E.J.!"

"I'm here, Cope." The answer from the velvet voice was so familiar he would recognize it anywhere.

She entered his field of vision, coming closer. As his sight became sharper, he drank in the rugged yet delicate beauty of her oval face with the high cheekbones and the liquid brown eyes. He relaxed, at peace. So much was uncertain. How long was I out? How bad was the wound? What happened to that kid? But everything was all right now. E.J. was here. She'll fill in the blanks.

She leaned over him, quietly pressed her face to his and kissed him on the forehead.

"How do you feel?"

"Like shit."

"Yeah, you look like that." She gave a slight smile.

Oh, that smile, it could melt a mountain. He chuckled at her frankness, wincing because any movement, even minor, increased the pain tenfold. In a second, when he recovered from that, he tried to ask an intelligent question, but his tongue did not cooperate, and it came out as gibberish. E.J. reached past him and came back with a half-full glass of water. Ever so gently, she lifted his head and expertly applied the rim of the glass to his dry, cracked lips. She rationed sips of the liquid to avoid choking him. He allowed her to lead him through this exercise until he had consumed a small amount, enough to wet his mouth and throat so they could function more normally.

"How long—long—was I out?" he asked as she lowered his head to the pillow. His voice still came out a coarse whisper, but his tongue was now able to form lucid words.

"Two days."

He took a second to process that and then moved on. "How bad is it?"

"What?"

"The wound. How bad is it?"

"You should rest now. We'll talk later."

He got that she was reluctant to talk about it. The pain apparent in her face told him that, but he had to know. "No. Now. I got to know."

"The doctor dug a forty-four slug out of your chest. You could have died, Cope."

Tears welled up in her eyes.

"I didn't," he said, intending to allay her concerns.

"Not for the want of trying," she said sarcastically.

She bit her lower lip to fight back those feelings that were just below the surface and were forcing their way up. He caught that and dropped the subject. His weakness took hold, demanding that he rest, but he was where he needed to be, with the one who loved him, and that made it all right. Closing his eyes, he allowed sleep to rush in and consume him.

———

WHEN HE NEXT AWAKENED, UNTOLD HOURS later, the room was dark. Must be night, he guessed. He was alone in the bed. That was not right. E.J. should be beside him, sleeping. He looked around. She sat in a chair gazing out the back window. Moving a little against the sheets, he made enough noise in the dead quiet to draw her attention.

She rose from the chair and went to the bed, to his side, crouching so her face was close to his. "Hungry?"

The question brought hunger to mind. "Yeah."

A little more of his voice had returned.

"I'll get you something." She moved to get up.

"I can wait. Must be late."

"No," she said as she rose, "you need your strength to heal. I'll get you something."

She left the room and returned a few minutes later with a bowl and a spoon. Sitting on the side of the bed, she fed him. If anyone else did this, he would be embarrassed. But E.J. doing it seemed natural. What did not seem natural was her manner—her coolness, her distance, at the same time that she was close.

Something was off.

"Something's chawing at you. What is it?" he asked when he was finished eating.

She smiled slightly. "Nothing. I'm just tired."

Her words did not convince him. But, due in part to his current weakened state, as well as a desire to refrain from upsetting E.J. further, he let it go, promising himself to pursue it at a more opportune time. Putting the bowl aside, she rounded the bed and placed herself ever so gently beside him, making him content, for the present.

———

HALFWAY INTO THE NEXT DAY, HE opened his eyes and, for the first time since the incident, he was fully awake. His mind actually functioned. The memories started.

He ran as fast as he could. Still, he was not gaining on the younger, more agile man he chased. At forty-three, he was not in the sort of condition required to engage in a footrace. Any running he had to do was usually done from the back of a horse, but that was not possible right now. This called for him to push his body to the maximum to overtake and apprehend this criminal. And it did not go his way. At the highest speed he could muster, he barely kept up with his quarry as they raced through the streets of Las Cruces.

Having been city marshal of this town for the last three years, Cope was finally in a maintenance position. Coming out of the Army after fighting the Comanche for more years than he liked to remember, he had done mustang work and then moved on to law enforcement jobs in several wide-open frontier towns. Those posts had required him to put his life on the line more often than he felt was healthy, but he had taken an oath and was determined to see it through. Cope's nature allowed no less.

He had followed this course for many years until E.J. happened. Edwina Justine Nettleton was her full name but she preferred—actually demanded—to be called E.J. She hated her name and had a formidable enough presence that no one questioned her.

Cope came upon her while returning from delivering a felon to the territorial prison. E.J. was on the trail of a horse thief when he met her. He threw in with her to attempt to run down the offender and retrieve her stolen horse. After successfully capturing the outlaw and liberating the animal, he began calling on E.J. They had an affinity for horses in common. He'd rounded up and sold wild horses for a time. She had raised and trained them. As time progressed, they found more things in common and realized that they needed to be together.

Marriage was the next step, and that's what changed Cope. He became more responsible, more careful with his life and limb and, because of that, he sought out a more peaceful town in which to work. Having settled on Las Cruces, he'd offered his services as city marshal and the town accepted him. That was three years ago, years that had been relatively calm and quiet with very little lawlessness and the resultant risk of the enforcer's life.

Aside from sucking the wind out of Cope, this current situation showed no signs of becoming life threatening. He was sure he would eventually run this stupid kid down and arrest him, and that would be that.

It had been a chance occurrence, this rob and run. Cope had been making his afternoon rounds and was about to step into Lassiter's Emporium to purchase a horehound stick to gnaw on while he walked. As he entered the open doorway, a figure abruptly appeared before him, moving fast. Cope collided with the stranger and was pushed back by the force of the impact.

Recovering quickly, he caught a fleeting glimpse of the assailant and identified him as a young man he had seen around town lately. In an instant, the man brushed past and took off on a dead run down the street as a shout came from inside the store. *"Stop that kid! He's a thief!"* It was the unmistakably high-pitched voice of Jules Lassiter, the owner.

As Lassiter ran toward the doorway, the call kicked Cope into action. He was running when his foot first hit the ground and, after a chase through a quarter of the town, he was still going.

A lean man with long legs, Cope's body was willing but his lungs were out of shape for this kind of sustained movement. He forced himself to exert extra effort but found that he could do no more than maintain the distance between himself and the fleeing suspect. As his breath began to falter, the kid rounded a corner, almost losing his footing, and made directly for the big door of the livery stable. Cope stayed with him and, watching him swing the door open and run inside, made for that opening.

Clearing the doorway, Cope stopped short and looked to his left to see Willy, the short, elderly livery manager, standing in the doorway to the office. He was scratching his head in confusion, having seen the young man dart past him into the stall area.

"Willy!" Cope shouted, almost breathless, "Get out of here! Go!"

Willy started moving when Cope gave the order and waved his left hand toward the street. As he hurried past, Cope dropped his hands to his knees and doubled over, trying to catch his wind. After a second of this—still breathing much harder than he was comfortable with—he proceeded forward. By this time, though, the suspect had disappeared somewhere ahead.

Aware that the building had no back door, Cope advanced carefully. Of the better than a dozen stalls, only a few showed the presence of animals, the rest being the most likely hiding places. Cope stopped at the beginning of the row and took his first quiet breath.

"I'm the marshal here, boy," he said in a deep voice with a distinct Southern twang, "You'd best show yourself 'fore this turns ugly."

No response. Cope began moving very slowly toward the first empty enclosure, his hand resting on the butt of the gun on his hip. Staying to the right of the center aisle allowed him to see well into the left stall before he arrived at the one on the right. With a quick movement, he glanced left, then stepped into the right-side enclosure to find this one empty as well. Horses occupied the next few but, not discounting the dumb factor, he moved toward them carefully on the off chance that the kid had risked joining an animal in close quarters. His quick examination proved this was not the case.

As Cope moved on, a quick movement from the next left-hand stall came as the young man moved from behind the enclosure with a gun in his hand. Giving no warning, he raised the weapon, cocked it and fired it point blank at Cope's middle as his mind processed the sight before him and reacted by lifting his own Colt. Too late! The kid's bullet slammed into his left shoulder just below the collar bone, knocking him back against the corner post of the stall behind him. A split second later, the resultant pain bit at him terribly. Managing to get his handgun clear of the holster, his attempt to defend himself was negated by his wobbly legs as shock and pain took over. The post prevented him from falling back but his legs sagged and he began sinking uncontrollably to the floor. Restarted after a long second of processing what he had just done, the kid darted past him and headed for the doorway.

Cope's legs went out in front of him, winding him up on his butt against the post. Realizing that he was beginning to pass out and that this boy had just become a potential killer, he raised the pistol and pulled back the hammer. If the kid made it out the door, he would be gone and any number of people would be in danger. This had to work. As his target crossed toward the doorway, he leveled his sights on center mass and pulled the trigger. The last thing he viewed before the veil of black took over was the suspect falling forward—then there was nothingness.

E.J. filled in the rest for him, explaining that Willy had gone back into the livery when he was sure the shooting had stopped and had found Cope up against the post. Willy also told her that he found the man who shot Cope with a bullet in his side that wound up in his innards. He asked after the condition of the man and she told him he'd died while being carried to the doctor's office. Although Cope was contrite about killing the offender, E.J. was not. She said no more on the subject.

———

THE NEXT FEW WEEKS WERE TOUGH on Cope. He was not comfortable with being waited on hand and foot. Accustomed to being active, he brooded during long hours of doing nothing but allowing the healing process to continue. During this time, E.J. busied herself all day and into the night, feeding him, keeping the wound clean, changing the bandage as well as keeping house and tending to the stock. The business, the horse training enterprise that she had continued after their marriage, demanded time and effort which she continued to put forth. All this told on her. Cope took note of it and tried to do for himself, but weakness and clumsiness prevailed, forcing him to relent and let E.J. do for him.

The doctor, after several visits, judged Cope's healing to be proceeding well, unusually well, truth be told. At the last such examination, he inquired as to when he would be able to go back to work. The doctor predicted at least several months, but cautioned that Cope's own body would govern the when of it. Looking past the doctor as the man answered the query, Cope caught the expression on E.J.'s face. He had to address this situation before it festered any further.

As the doctor departed, E.J. walked out to the barn to tend her horses. That was her excuse, but, to Cope, it was not true. Whatever this is, it's eating her up. He stepped out of the house and the sun on his weather-beaten face made him keenly aware of the amount of time he had been confined indoors. Steadying himself, he carefully followed her to the barn, entering as she approached one of the stalls.

"E.J.," he said softly.

She stopped but did not turn.

"You shouldn't be out here," she said, almost coldly. "Go back inside."

"You haven't been yourself since I got shot. Whatever's bothering you is driving a goddamn wedge between us. It needs to stop. Tell me. What's on your mind?"

E.J. turned slowly, deliberately. Finally, a scowl on her face replaced the false smile.

"You, Cope," she said, "you, dead. That's what's on my mind. You could have died. Two inches to the right and that bullet would have plugged your heart. Now you want to go back to it, to take more chances that could get you shot again? I can't bear it, Cope. I just can't."

"I didn't die. And I'm not going to."

Now, once started, the flood gates opened. Tears streamed down E.J.'s cheeks and her face scrunched up in torment. "You don't know that, Cope! You don't know that!"

Her shouting startled the horses, making them stamp nervously in their stalls.

"You put that badge back on, you don't know when the next son of a bitch pulls a gun on you. Next time, maybe it's fatal. Maybe you do die. What am I supposed to do then? I don't want to bury you."

She unleashed that which had been pent up since the incident first happened. Truth be told, since long before that. Remarkably, though speaking through tears, she held it together and made her case intelligently, albeit emotionally. Touched by this, Cope moved closer to her and took her in his arms, forcing his left arm to mimic his right arm even though pain and stiffness were still present. Sobbing, she did not respond in kind but kept talking. She had started this now and she was determined to get it all out.

"We've got something very special, Cope. Maybe you haven't noticed, but our love is very special. Not many people I know have what we have. And I refuse to give that up. Las Cruces can damn well find another marshal. Just not you. I won't have it. I won't give you back to them. You're mine and I won't give you back. I love you too much and I want you safe."

"I love you, too, and I am safe. This is the safest, quietest town I could find. What happened could have happened anywhere. There's less chance here than somewhere else."

She found his reasoning flawed.

"If you're not wearing the badge, not putting yourself in the line of fire, it won't happen at all."

"I took an oath, E.J. I can't just walk away from that."

"And the promise you made when you married me, what about that? Would you walk away from that?"

"Course not. I love you."

"And I love you. But I told you, I won't give you back to them. If you force me to do that, I... I'll leave you. I swear it, Cope. I'll leave you. I'd rather be without you than to have to bury you. I couldn't bear that. I won't."

This stunned him. He stared at the determined look on her face. She meant every word of it. E.J. did not talk for the sake of talking. Whatever she said was the result of deep thought and consideration.

"I had no idea you felt like this," he said.

"I think I always felt this way. From the first time I knew I loved you, I wanted you safe. I tried to tell myself I should support you and let you do what you wanted, dangerous or not. But, when you got shot, that all changed. It all became clear. Your dying went from a remote possibility to a definite fact in the time it took for that bullet to rip its way into you. I swore, then and there, I'd do everything I could to prevent that from happening again."

"I had no idea."

"I know. I kept it hidden until now. But I can't anymore. You wanted to know what's on my mind? Well, that's it. I've resolved myself to it. I will leave you, Cope, if you go back to that life. I will. I mean it."

She pulled herself from him and turned away, succumbing to the emotions that now took over. He took a moment to let this sink in. She was dead serious. He realized also that, although she was asking him to completely alter his life, he would do anything to keep her from leaving him.

He moved closer to her and put his hand on her shoulder. "I know you do. I don't want you to leave."

She sniffed back her tears. "I don't want to, but—"

"I'll resign. I'll talk to the mayor tomorrow."

"You will?"

"You're the best thing that ever happened to me. Nothing's ever going to come between us. I'm sorry I put you through this. I just didn't know."

She turned to him and he folded her into his arms. Her arms went around him in response.

"I tried, Cope. I really tried. But I just can't anymore."

"You don't have to. It's settled."

They continued holding each other in the embrace. Right now, nothing else mattered but their love. Cope resolved to preserve that love.

2

COPE CONTEMPLATED THE TWO PINHOLES IN his leather vest where the marshal's badge had been positioned for the past three years. It was hard to believe that the garment was that old but he reckoned he had purchased it just prior to their arrival in Las Cruces. He had worn the thing constantly since that time. The badge had always resided in the same spot and the wear around the holes showed that to be true. Now, it was gone. Just like that, no longer Marshal Worley, but plain Cope Worley, unemployed citizen.

Seated in a rocking chair on his front porch, he looked up from the vest to resume watching E.J. who was engaged in training a big black stallion in the corral adjacent to the barn. Impressed anew at her ability to communicate with this horse in particular—and almost every other horse in general—he watched as she used hand signals, never touching the horse. She put the animal through its paces—rearing on cue, bowing and kneeling as well as shaking its head in the affirmative when offered a carrot. Yes, sir, she's got a real way with horses.

His eyes on her drew E.J.'s attention. Some time had passed since he'd turned in his badge. He was most likely bored out of his mind. A glance his way made her even more certain her assumption was correct. Patting the nose of the big black gently, she strode to the corral gate and let herself out.

Her eyes stayed on Cope through the entire walk. Even slumped in that chair, he looks impressive. The broad shoulders, the tallness of him, the square jaw, the dark, penetrating eyes, the silver hair, all add up to my Cope, my protector, my rock. He would do whatever was necessary to keep her safe, and she swore to God she would do the same. She fleetingly wondered what she would have done if she had never met him. Discarding this, she concentrated on his current presence and her oath to leave him to keep from burying him. It had been a chance she took voicing that ultimatum, but she had been prepared to walk away if he did not comply. That would have been the next best thing to his acquiescence, and the only other thing she could live with, for she could not bear him dying. His submission to her wishes made her very happy, but now, she had to be certain that his next endeavor, whatever that might be, would make him equally satisfied.

Cope watched as she approached him. He had done exactly as he said he would, going the next day to see the mayor and resigning his position. The act was initially not well received, but after a statement of his reasons, he convinced the man he would not reconsider. Upon his return home, he took to the rocking chair and stayed there until now. His eyes followed E.J. as she stepped onto the porch and crouched beside him.

"You're not going to sit there for the rest of your life, are you?" she asked.

"You'll have that pony eating out of your hand right soon."

His statement was an obvious attempt to avoid the subject. He had no job and he needed one. Well aware of the fact, he did not need to be reminded of it.

"Never mind the pony. You're not getting off that easy."

She was both serious and flippant at the same time.

"We both know you've got to figure out what you're going to do, and sitting here rocking is not getting that done."

"I know," he replied, "but I have been pondering. You might not like what I came up with."

"What's that?"

"Thinking of going back to chasing mustangs. Not breaking them, mind you. Don't reckon these old bones can handle that. Just rounding them up and selling them. Less money, but still a living. Less hard knocks as well."

"Why do you think I'd be against that?"

"Well, I reckon we'd have to move. There's no market in these parts for mustangs. I checked on that. We'd have to go where the market is."

"And where's that?"

She was showing *some* interest, at least. This encouraged him to continue. "The day I resigned, I sent a telegram to Rud Tanner. He's the sheriff down in Senado Pass, down by Laredo. Think I mentioned him a time or two. Anyway, I asked him about the market for mustangs down there. I'm waiting for his answer."

She was a little disconcerted by her husband's tactics. "I see. When were you going to tell me about this?"

"When I got Rud's answer. Not fond of telling half stories."

"And I'm not fond of being kept in the dark."

He smiled. "So, you good with it?"

"I can do what I do anywhere," she replied. "When will you have his answer?"

Cope turned playful in an attempt to lighten the mood.

"When he sends it." He pushed the back of his hat forward so the front covered his forehead and most of his eyes. She chewed on her bottom lip.

"There's a name for people like you...." She allowed the statement to trail off.

"Yeah?"

She rose, somewhat frustrated, and started back toward the corral. "Never mind."

———

WITHIN TWO DAYS, THE LOCAL TELEGRAPH office delivered the answer to Cope's query. As the delivery boy rode off, Cope stood at the corral fence and read the message to E.J. *"Forty-six ranches in these parts need constant supply of horses. Also, stable in town for sale. If interested, wire deposit for option on stable straightaway."*

"Wonder how big the stable is?"

"Don't reckon it matters. We buy it, we can make it whatever we want it to be."

"Sounds good," she said with a smile.

Cope pushed his hat so it sat on the back of his head. "Reckon I'll be sending that deposit today."

With E.J.'s help, he hitched horses to the buckboard they used to lay in supplies and drove to town. Once there, he telegraphed the deposit and a separate message to Rud Tanner which authorized Tanner to place the deposit on the facility. He requested the total price and terms of the deal as well. While waiting for the reply, he visited the doctor to make certain that he could make the trip to Senado Pass should his offer be accepted. The doctor, while issuing a caution against overdoing things, allowed as how it had been several months— sufficient time for healing—and gave him a conditional clean bill of health.

By nightfall, Tanner's telegram arrived, indicating the price and the requirement that the balance be paid within two weeks. Cope wired the funds immediately with instructions to consummate the deal. He also informed Tanner that they would proceed to Senado Pass just as soon as they could make the arrangements.

Cope and E.J. lost no time packing up what they could fit in the buckboard. The excess they allowed to remain in place. With their horses in tow behind the wagon, they set out two days later for Senado Pass, stopping in Las Cruces to consign their holdings to the bank for sale to the highest bidder.

—

FACED WITH A GRUELING SIX-HUNDRED-fifty-mile journey southeast into Texas, they followed the course of the Rio Grande down past El Paso and stayed with the river until it began to dip almost due south. Veering to stay in a southeasterly direction, they continued until they again picked up the Rio Grande in the vicinity of San Felipe Del Rio. Thereafter, they tracked the Rio Grande to Laredo where they secured final directions. Senado Pass was situated about ten miles northeast of Laredo's eastern boundary.

As they approached the town, Cope observed the flat rolling plains of cattle country. There was no doubt about it, horses would be needed in constant supply to work the ranches in the area. His knowing smile told E.J. they had indeed made the right decision. Though exhausted from the rigors of the trail, they pressed on in the last leg of the journey with renewed energy.

Their inauspicious entrance into Senado Pass was made in late afternoon with the sun beginning to wane at their backs. The trip from Laredo took from early morning until then.

It appeared to be a sleepy village, mostly made up of old adobe buildings with newer wooden affairs sprinkled throughout. A typical southwest Texas cow town, it was a sight with which Cope was all too familiar. He had served as a peace officer in many similar locations.

E.J.'s reaction was mixed. While she was apprehensive about the size and the attributes of the town, she remembered Rud Tanner's statement about the ranches in the area and was somewhat heartened by Cope's confident smile. Not one to make snap judgments, she resigned herself to wait and see what developed.

Their entrance into Senado Pass was by the main street, a wide, dirt covered road that boasted no boardwalks save for the porches of many of the buildings. This appeared to make a simple walk difficult as one would need to ascend and descend each structure individually or walk the dirt street. While the layout of the town was haphazard at best, most of the businesses were lined along both sides of that street. Residences and some smaller enterprises were scattered about on either side of the key thoroughfare with no discernible organization and no direct way of locating particular establishments or homes.

A quarter of the way down the street, they noticed an unoccupied stable on their right. It was a somewhat rundown affair, not bounded on either side by neighboring buildings. Cope pointed. "Appears to be what we came for."

"It needs work," E.J. said.

"Yep."

They continued past the stable as Cope searched both sides of the street for the sheriff's office or some identifiable equivalent which might house Rud Tanner. They found it toward the end of the street, a tiny structure of clapboard with steel bars covering the windows. It was not bounded by any other shops for several yards around. Above the door, a wooden sign with black lettering identifying it as the sheriff's office and jail was suspended by ropes from a stout pole that jutted out perpendicularly from the front wall. They turned toward the building.

"Now, don't be put off too much by Rud. He's got a foul mouth and he's every bit of a slob. Likely could use a bath as well, if memory serves, but you surely won't have a better man beside you in a fight."

"What fight is that?"

Cope grinned. "Figure of speech."

He pulled the team to a stop in front of the place and tied the reins off on the brake handle. Climbing down from the seat, he reached up to help E.J. and winced at the slight persistent pain still present in his left shoulder area. She noticed his reaction and waved off his assistance in favor of fending for herself. They proceeded to the door and entered, finding Rud Tanner seated behind a table facing the door with his legs stretched from the chair to the tabletop.

A slender, wiry man with a long, wide face and small, dark eyes, there appeared to be a perpetual smile on his wide lips below a broad nose. On his jutting chin, he grew a vague attempt at a goatee that was overshadowed by several days growth of beard. Almost bald, his dark hair was unkempt and desperately needed soap and water. Indeed, that necessity spread to his entire body and the resultant odor told that tale quite vividly. The fact that his collarless shirt and saddle pants had not been washed in longer than recently added to the olfactory assault.

"Howdy, Rud," Cope said, looking past the man's mud encrusted boots.

Immediately recognizing his friend, Tanner pulled his feet from the table to the floor and came upright in the chair.

"Well, Cope Worley, you old horse thief! How the f—" He stopped short of the expletive at the sudden sight of E.J. stepping in behind Cope and coming into full view. His smile broadened as he came around the table. "Well, shit, Cope, y'all didn't never tell me you done married such a looker." Turning his attention to E.J., he bowed rather ungracefully as he said, "Rudford Tanner, at your service, ma'am."

E.J. smiled and stepped forward, enduring the smell of the man as she tried to maintain courtesy.

"How do you do, Mr. Tanner." She flashed him a sincere smile.

Trying to be gentlemanly and to control his cursing at the same time, Tanner stumbled verbally.

"Shit—eh—Shoot, ma'am, it's just Rud, just Rud is all."

E.J.'s next words put him at ease.

"I'm happy to meet you, Rud. I'm E.J."

"You surely are, ma'am. You surely are. Hell, Cope, I about give up on y'all. Been over a month, ain't it?"

"Wasn't about to kill the horses getting here," Cope said flatly.

"Well, that's mighty well told. It's surely good to see you and to meet your beautiful wife."

It was obvious, now, that Tanner had collected himself.

"Good to see you, too," Cope replied. "Thanks for what you did. I won't forget it."

"Ain't nothing. What are friends for? Say, y'all just get in?"

Receiving an affirmative answer from his visitors, Tanner continued. "Must be hungry then. Let's get us a bite at the cantina, then I'll show y'all the stable."

It was dusk when they finished their meal. Conversation had run the gamut from Tanner describing his first meeting with Cope in a wide-open Kansas cow town and their subsequent exploits in combating the lawless element there, to Cope relating how he and E.J. met. It also, briefly, covered Cope's wound and resignation.

Tanner escorted E.J. up the street to the stable while Cope climbed aboard the wagon and turned the team in that same direction. Their entrance into the establishment brought recent memories back to Cope, since it was laid out in a similar pattern to the livery in Las Cruces which had hosted the shooting.

"It's a tad run down. I'll give you that," Tanner said.

Cope and E.J. made a cursory examination.

"Nothing that can't be made right," Cope replied.

"The owner done signed the deed over to you," Tanner said when he was certain they were satisfied. "Got it back in the office. Y'all can record it in Laredo when you got a mind to. Once that's done, you got yourself a stable."

"I want to add my thanks, Rud," E.J. said. "This came at a perfect time."

"Glad I could help," Tanner replied. "Well, I got to be getting back. All them laws to enforce and the like. Give me a holler, you need anything, hear?"

Cope and E.J. both thanked him as he turned for the big main doorway. Half-way there, he turned with a look of curiosity on his face.

"Say, Cope, you never done said why you give up the badge like you done."

Cope glanced at E.J. "It's a long story, Rud."

"And not one for telling," E.J. said.

Her expression warned Tanner off the subject. He smiled, shrugged and continued his exit.

———

COPE DROVE THE WAGON INSIDE THE stable. He and E.J. placed the animals in individual stalls and cared for them. After an uncomfortable night's sleep in blanket rolls on the floor of the stable's office, they set to work repairing and sprucing up the interior of the establishment. Within the next few days, Cope took the wagon to Laredo and purchased split logs necessary to build a corral behind the stable. While there, he recorded the deed at the county land office, making the property officially his.

The corral took a couple of weeks to complete, even with the occasional help of Rud Tanner. The back-breaking work told Cope his age was catching up with him and that the aches and pains from the near fatal wound would remain a permanent addition to his existence. He was grateful for the help provided by E.J. and his friend.

Cope responded favorably to Tanner's requests for assistance. He would occupy the sheriff's office during periods when Tanner was called away. Slowly, these sessions became more frequent, reaching a point at which Tanner offered him the post of special temporary deputy. He accepted the task as a way of meeting his obligation to Tanner for all his assistance.

After several weeks of building, repairing, and sleeping on the office floor, Cope decided it was time to find some horses to sell to start an income flow. His desires to either build or purchase a house and to get shed of uncomfortable nights drove this deed. E.J. wholeheartedly agreed. He set out on his first mustang search in more years than he really cared to remember.

At mid-morning on the day Cope left, E.J. strode determinedly up the street to Tanner's office and entered to find the sheriff in the same position he had occupied on their initial meeting. At the sight of her and the serious expression on her face, he came to his feet sharply.

"How do, E.J. What can I do you for?"

"Cope left this morning to scout mustangs," she said, obviously concerned about something.

"Yep, he done told me he was heading out."

E.J. stepped closer. "What was your intention in giving Cope that badge? He's renounced that life."

"I don't know. He seems bound and determined to pay back what he thinks he owes me, I just reckoned he could get paid a mite whilst he's doing it, is all."

"That better be the all of it, Mr. Tanner. Cope won't tell you this, but I will. That bullet almost took him from me. When he recovered, I told him I would leave him if he didn't turn in his badge. He agreed. Now, if you have any intention of pulling him back into that life, you need to rethink that. Believe me, you don't want to get on my bad side."

He studied her for a moment and cracked a nervous smile. "No, Mrs. Worley, I can see that would not be too comforting. I swear to you, I had no intent on doing nothing but getting Cope some cash. I seen him look at you when I asked him about why he quit. And I seen the look you give him. I surely do not want to get betwixt them looks. Far as I'm concerned, he ain't doing nothing more than sitting here in this here chair when I ain't, if'n that's acceptable to you."

"As long as that's as far as it goes, it's all right. But know this— I'll fight tooth and nail to make sure Cope stays safe. And *mine.*"

Tanner nodded firmly. "Yes, ma'am, I believe you. I surely do. And mighty well told."

3

T HE WATERS OF THE RIO GRANDE were calm during a particularly dark night, as a small canoe made its way quietly across the river from the Mexican side toward a sloping rise that led to the streets of Laredo. On board, a lone figure worked the paddle as silently as possible to prevent detection as the vessel sliced through the water in an almost straight line from shore to shore. Only the gentle sloshing of fluid disrupted by the paddling disturbed the quiet. While the night was silent enough to allow this to be discerned, unless one purposely listened for the sound, it went unnoticed. The occupant depended on this to remain unobserved but still tried to keep the noise to an absolute minimum.

Hunkered into the canoe to present the smallest possible presence, the man was almost imperceptible under the huge dark sombrero. He directed the boat toward the shore and gave a final push on the paddle to force the bow to lodge itself in the wet sand, bringing it to an abrupt halt. Taking a second to be certain there were no observers, he stood and balanced himself as he made his way from the stern to the bow and stepped onto the bank and the relative safety of the United States. He shoved the bow of the canoe off the bank to drift aimlessly downstream. Retaining the paddle, he dug his sandaled feet into the rough sand and climbed the steep grade to the level of the dirt above.

Halfway up, movement caught his eye and caused him to stop and crouch. Approaching from the left on the road that formed at the top of the slope, a rider eased his horse along. He carried a rifle that he held by the fore grip while the butt rested in the crook between his hip and leg. The horse walked as the rider scanned the area from the river to his location. Unseen, the climber waited tensely as the horseman passed, observing the dark clothing and the polished boots that told him this was most likely a U. S. Army soldier patrolling the border. Remaining in that position, he waited until the image could no longer be seen and the sounds of the horse's hooves faded away. Only then did he continue his ascent.

As light from the streets beyond reached him, his face became partially visible. Although covered by a thick overgrowth of beard, the big, dark eyes and thick lips could be made out under the shadowy cover of the sombrero. Wearing peasant clothing, he had wrapped himself in a colorful, faded serape from shoulder to mid-calf. Only the hand clutching the paddle remained visible from under the blanket.

Glancing around cautiously, he satisfied himself that he was alone and proceeded toward the lights and activity. Reaching the streets, he kept to the shadows and watched for an opportunity to execute the next step in his plan.

From a position inside an alley between two office buildings, he observed his target. A well-dressed man of about his own height and weight approached on the street. Obviously intoxicated, he weaved and staggered his way to and past the alleyway. The man in the sombrero stealthily exited the passageway behind his quarry and hurried to a striking position behind him. He raised the paddle above his head, allowing the sombrero to be pushed off his head as the serape dropped behind him.

He swung forcefully at the head of the drunk. The instrument connected with a crack, hitting the man behind the ear and pitching him forward in an immediately stunned state. As he sagged to the ground, his attacker swooped in behind him, clutched one arm and dragged him back into the alley. He hurriedly darted back into the street to retrieve the victim's black silk top hat and his own sombrero and blanket. Returning to the alley, he observed the man stirring back to consciousness. Dropping the hat, he draped the man's body with the serape from throat to shoes. He proceeded to deliver a series of blows with the paddle to the wounded man's head and face until he was certain there was no sign of life remaining. He did this with no compunction or hesitation. To him, this was simply a matter of ensuring his own survival.

Within the next few minutes, he removed the blood-spattered cover from the body and used it to wrap the battered head to prevent blood from transferring to the dead man's clothing. He carefully removed the clothing and shoes and placed them a safe distance away from the body. Stripping off his own ragged clothes, he climbed into the dead man's outfit which consisted of a white shirt, black frock coat, and trousers. These things fit him well enough to be passable as his own. The shoes, on the other hand, were slightly larger than they should have been, but a good tug on the laces solved the problem enough to temporarily suffice. He placed the top hat on his head, allowing his abundantly curly hair to spill out the sides. Patting down the coat, he found a wallet in the inside pocket. Several documents within identified the owner as James Gant, an attorney residing and practicing in Laredo. Also, inside the wallet, he found one hundred five dollars in United States greenbacks. He could certainly use that.

So, at least for the present, he would cease to be Lorenzo Cholla, fugitive from Mexican justice, in favor of this new identity. He adjusted these strange clothes and assumed the posture he related to the station in life that an attorney would occupy and stepped forth into that life.

———

USING HIS ABILITY TO MIMIC ACCENTS and dialects combined with his knowledge of the English language, acquired from previous forays into this country, Cholla moved among the inhabitants of Laredo as an American attorney, James Gant, without detection. Intelligently gathering information from passersby, he located Gant's place of residence and determined that the man lived alone. Entering through an open window to avoid encountering anyone who might know Gant, he found, to his advantage, clothing and accessories as well as a bank book and several documents bearing Gant's signature. This would allow him, at least in the short term, to become Gant. He gathered the things he could carry and exited through the same window.

After locating a hiding place for the articles he had just obtained, Cholla moved to a different part of the city and took a room in an inexpensive rooming house using his new identity. Depositing his loot in the room, he spent several days perfecting Gant's signature and then went to the bank to withdraw Gant's savings. The forgery passed scrutiny, allowing him to clean out the account. His first purchase with his newly obtained funds was a Colt New Line .30 caliber pocket revolver and a shoulder rig to contain it.

For several weeks thereafter, Cholla, now considering himself well off financially, circulated within a better section of Laredo, passing himself off as James Gant. Spending most of his days in the rented room, he frequented night spots that featured gambling. He engaged in games of chance which, utilizing trickery, gained him even more funds. At the same time, he identified people who seemed likely targets and followed them to isolated points at which he could assault and rob them. None of these victims survived.

While the Marshal's Office investigated these violent deaths, Cholla moved freely, continuing to frequent the clubs at night while remaining secluded during the day.

Requesting entry into the Laredo Gentleman's Club, Cholla identified himself as James Gant. As he was admitted, an overweight, heavily mustached man stepped in front of him.

"Excuse me. Did I hear you identify yourself as James Gant?" the man demanded loudly.

"You did." Cholla replied quickly and openly.

The rotund man stared Cholla straight in the eye.

"Well, sir, I'm Walter Roseville and my partner, James Gant, has been missing for several weeks. You are an imposter." Roseville reached for Cholla's lapels in an attempt to grab them. "What have you done with Gant?"

Cholla moved quickly, throwing a clenched fist at Roseville's face and catching the man on the chin. As Roseville reeled from the blow, Cholla spun and made for the door. Before Roseville could recover, and before anyone else reacted to the altercation, Cholla cleared the door and disappeared into the night.

"Get the marshal!" Roseville shouted, holding his wounded chin, "That man's an imposter!"

Cholla ran for several blocks until he ascertained he was not being chased. Stopping to catch his breath, he realized his ruse had run its course. He returned to his room and packed a change of clothes. Leaving by the back door, he wandered the city until he located a livery stable with an unlocked door. Trying to avoid calling attention to himself by renting or buying a horse, he entered the stable and helped himself to an animal and outfit. After saddling the mount, he led it quietly out of the area before mounting and setting out to leave Laredo.

Riding northeast from Laredo, Cholla arrived the next day near a stagecoach relay station not far from Senado Pass. By now, he dressed in clothes more suitable for the trail. Fearful of traveling on a stolen horse in broad daylight, he decided on a different plan. Riding ahead on the main road for a short distance and noting the presence of coach tracks, he unsaddled the horse in the cover of some bushes and sent it on its way into the wilderness. With the saddle in hand, he stepped out onto the road and waited for the next coach to pass.

Half an hour into the vigil, the coach headed his way. Shouldering the saddle, he began walking in the same direction the coach traveled. Upon its approach, he turned and waved at the driver to stop. Pulling the six-in-hand team to a halt, the driver twitched his huge handlebar mustache and called out, "You got a problem, stranger?"

Immediately assuming a new persona to maintain his cover, Cholla replied in Spanish accented speech.

"Sí, Señor. My horse, she break a leg. I have to shoot her. Do you have room for me, *por favor?"*

"Coach is full up but you're welcome to ride up here with me, if'n you're a mind."

"Gracias."

Cholla moved quickly to a position below the driver and handed his saddle up to the man, then climbed up beside him as the saddle was deposited on the coach roof.

"Name's Hank," the driver said.

"I am Lorenzo Cholla," Cholla replied with a smile.

"Whereabouts you headed?"

"I will know that when I get there. Where are you going?"

"We're bound for Senado Pass, just up the line here."

"That will do for me. Thank you for your kindness."

"Ain't nothing. I'm obliged for the company. Gets a tad lonesome up here."

The driver called out to several of the team by name. In a few seconds, the coach resumed its journey.

———

IN THE FEW MONTHS SINCE COPE and E.J. had taken up residence in Senado Pass, their business thrived. After Cope's first foray into areas known to be populated by wild horses, he returned with a dozen head of prime animals. Having made contact with most of the ranchers in the area, he secured contracts with several to supply horses that could be broken to the saddle.

At the same time, E.J. maintained the stable and continued her training enterprise, selling off several of her previously trained charges and identifying future candidates from those Cope brought in from the field. With her ability to gentle a horse using only speech and touch, she never needed to physically domesticate them. By the time she placed saddles on their backs, they were at the point of doing her bidding and they tolerated the encumbrance with no arguments.

When he was not tracking mustangs, Cope helped with the operation of the stable and continued to fill in for Rud Tanner when needed. Tanner was careful to limit Cope's deputy duties to no more than jail-sitting, thus keeping his word to E.J.

Returning to town after delivering the last of his mustangs to one of the ranches, Cope immediately prepared for another trip. As he drew rein just outside the stable, she emerged with a pretty, white mare, leading the horse by the reins.

"You think she's ready?" Cope asked as he dismounted.

"We're going to find out right quick." she said.

"I'm heading back out. Another order to fill. Likely be gone before you get back."

"You be careful, Cope."

Cope nodded and watched as she stroked the mare's nose and whispered something to it. Then, with authority, she stepped to the horse's left side and set her foot in the stirrup. Remaining in that position for several seconds, she continued to whisper, then swung into the saddle in one smooth motion. The horse shuffled nervously. E.J. leaned over its neck and patted gently, still whispering. Then she sat straight in the saddle and gently pulled the left rein. Responding, the horse turned left and began moving up the street.

"I don't know how you do it."

E.J. smiled. "Nor do I."

Cope watched as she rode up the street and out of town. When he could no longer see her, he entered the stable, leading his horse. After caring for the animal, he selected another and saddled it. He prepared his traveling goods, saddled and loaded a packhorse and rode off in an entirely different direction.

E.J. rode for several miles, at differing speeds and over various terrains. The mare responded wonderfully, seeming to enjoy the journey almost as much as she did. During the trip, she crossed paths at a distance with the coach carrying Cholla. While she paid no attention to the conveyance, Cholla definitely noticed the rider and horse, noting the lines and the beauty of both.

Some time later, she entered the main street at a trot, catching sight of a stranger outside the stable. She noticed the saddle sitting on the ground next to him and found that curious.

Cholla watched her approach and recognized both the rider and horse. Admiring the attractiveness of both from a closer perspective, he smiled. E.J. reined in a few feet from him and dismounted. Her first action was to congratulate the horse with whispers and pats on the nose. The mare nickered pleasantly. She turned her attention to the stranger.

"*Buen día, Señorita,*" Cholla said, smiling and removing his hat, "I am Lorenzo Cholla, at your service."

"Good day to you, Mr. Cholla. I'm E.J. Worley. My husband and I run this stable."

"*Lo siento.* But of course, one of your beauty would be already spoken for."

Unaccustomed to Latin manners and a little disconcerted by his esteem, E.J. sought to get to the point of his visit. "What can I do for you, Mr. Cholla?"

"I need to purchase a horse. My own broke a leg on the trail and I was forced to shoot her."

"I'm sorry you had to do that. I wondered about the saddle. I do have horses for sale. They're inside."

Cholla moved instead to the white mare. "Such a beautiful animal," he said. "Is she fast?"

"Like the wind."

"I would have her. Is she for sale?"

"Well, I just finished training her," E.J. replied hesitantly, "but, yes, she's for sale."

"*Bueno,*" Cholla said decisively. "I will purchase her."

"You don't even know how much I'm asking."

"This is of no concern to me," Cholla said, gesturing grandly. "I will pay you whatever you feel is fair. I trust you."

E.J. thought for a second.

"All things considered then, I'd need forty dollars to let her go."

"*Bueno.* I will pay you forty dollars."

"Mr. Cholla, you just bought yourself a horse. Why don't you come back in an hour? I'll groom her, feed her, and have the bill of sale ready. You can leave your saddle there if you like."

"*Mil gracias, Señora* Worley. A pleasure."

As Cholla walked away, E.J. experienced an inexplicable sense that there was something off about this stranger. Shrugging this away, she led the mare inside for care and feeding. In about an hour, Cholla returned to find E.J. in the office at the desk. She looked up as he entered.

"You're just in time," she said, fingering the pen. "I need some help spelling your name. Didn't want to get it wrong."

"Of course," he said as he rounded the desk. "I will write it for you."

She handed him the pen and pointed to the spot on the form that required his name. He talked as he wrote it. "The double 'l' is said like 'y', so it is Cho-ya."

"Thank you. The mare's ready."

Cholla reached into his pants pocket and brought out two twenty-dollar gold pieces.

"The payment." He placed the coins in her hand.

She rose and accompanied him into the stable where the mare stood bearing Cholla's rig.

"She responds better to gentleness," E.J. said.

"As do most women. I promise I will never abuse her. We will become great friends."

He extended his hand and she shook it.

"It was a pleasure meeting you," he said cordially. "I hope to see you again."

"I'll be around."

He picked up the reins and mounted. With a kissing sound, he put the mare in motion. They rode out of the stable and up the street slowly. E.J. watched him go and again experienced the uneasiness that there was more to this stranger than met the eye.

4

RUD TANNER WORE A CHANGE OF clothes. This was evident as he stepped out of his office at midmorning. While the garments were just as worn, they were clean, as was his person. With his conversion revolver on his hip and carrying a Winchester rifle, he seemed somewhat more on his game than usual. He strode confidently toward the bank.

Seated in a chair across the street from Tanner, Lorenzo Cholla quietly observed, taking in every nuance of the view before him. He watched Tanner closely and took particular interest in the scene that played out prior to Tanner's arrival at the bank.

As Tanner advanced, he sighted a familiar figure. A young man of about his same height stood on the boardwalk leaning lazily against a building wall a few doors closer than the bank. From his distance, Cholla could not be certain, but the youth looked to be no more than eighteen-years-old. A handsome young man, he had a broad face with wide-set, squinty eyes and a pointed chin. Cholla noted the young man's outfit seemed to give the impression he was older. Not an unusual action for one that young. Too much in a hurry to grow up and unaware of how to go about it.

Tanner walked toward the boy, also noticing his bibbed prairie shirt and the striped britches that attempted to portray an imposing figure. He was more concerned, however, with the low-slung holster belt containing the Colt handgun. Told him to put that thing away. Coming to within four feet, Tanner stopped and glared at the kid.

"Billy, I done told you I don't want you on the street wearing that piece," Tanner said. "You got a hearing problem?"

"I'm just standing here, Sheriff. Ain't bothering nobody."

Billy's voice was higher than he would have preferred, and his words came out in a sing-song pattern, but they did not sit well with Tanner all the same.

"You bother *me*," Tanner said. "So, you just be standing there somewheres else, away from me. And get shed of that gun 'fore I run you in on general principles. Now git!"

Billy started to move, then turned to face Tanner. "You know, Sheriff, one of these days, you going to get me mad."

He was trying to sound tough, but it didn't work with Tanner. "You want to talk about mad, kid?" He took another step closer. "You go ahead on and get me mad. Then you'll find out about mad, and then some. Now you take that damned hog leg off and you get your ass the hell out of my sight!"

Billy stood his ground, for all of a few seconds, while Tanner stared him down. Then he stepped off the boardwalk and started across the street. As he walked, he unbuckled the holster belt and removed it from his waist. Tanner watched closely until he was certain the kid was no longer a threat, then he continued toward the bank. Reckon someday I'll likely have to deal with Billy for good and all. But it would not happen today. There were other things to handle this day.

Curious, and interested on more than one level, Cholla rose

from his chair as Billy stepped up on the sidewalk a few feet from his location.

"Mi joven, amigo!"

Billy stopped and turned. While the voice was unfamiliar, and the call seemed pleasant enough, he still remained guarded, a result of his encounter with the sheriff. "You calling me, Mister?"

Cholla approached. *"Sí."* Only when he reached the boy did he continue. "Why does this sheriff treat you with such disrespect?" His question was asked with forced concern for Billy's feelings and well-being. It was meant to open a dialogue and it accomplished its purpose.

"He don't like me," Billy said. "Thinks I'm a troublemaker."

"Surely, even a stranger such as I can see he is mistaken. You are much more of a man than he. I can tell that."

"You reckon so?"

"Oh, *sí*. Of course. In every way."

"Well, mighty nice of you to say so, Mister—eh."

"Cholla. I am Lorenzo Cholla."

"Billy Griff, that's me. Maybe you heard of me."

"I am sad to say I have not, Billy Griff. But I have just arrived here. And now I will listen for your name to be spoken."

"Well, thanks, Mr. Cholla. I'm sure you'll hear it."

"As am I, Billy. Well, I will not detain you. I merely found that man's treatment of you distasteful and I wanted you to know that I was offended to witness it."

"Damn decent of you."

"Think nothing of it, Billy. *Buen día.*"

"And to you, Mr. Cholla."

Billy tipped his hat cordially and went on his way, a smile broadening on his face. Cholla, satisfied that he had made an impressionable first contact that would be developed further when necessary, returned to his chair to continue his vigil.

Tanner reached the bank and stopped outside. As he stood, obviously waiting for something, he pulled out his pocket watch and checked the time, then he continued waiting.

After several minutes, a stagecoach drawn by a six-in-hand team rolled into the street and came to a halt in front of the bank. On board was a driver as well as a shotgun guard. Behind it, two rifle guards pulled up and dismounted. At the same time, the guard alighted from the coach seat. They came together on the side of the coach where Sheriff Tanner joined them. Once they all shook hands, one of the guards opened the door to the coach and lifted out a metal strongbox secured by a stout padlock. Immediately, the four men walked the box into the building.

Cholla continued to observe the exercise, noting that the coach was identified by the markings on its side—*Wells, Fargo & Co.* He recalled that the coach which had brought him to Senado Pass was locally run, not operated by Wells Fargo. Also, of interest was the fact that there were no passengers present here. This appeared to be a special run set up solely to deliver this strongbox, obviously containing something of great value, directly to the bank.

Understanding that he was unprepared at this point to act on this information, he questioned the consistency and the frequency of this operation as well as the contents of the box. Further observation would be required before formulating any kind of a plan to acquire whatever the box held. He noted the day of the week and the time of day on which this occurred, fully intending to continue monitoring events involving the bank in general and these deliveries in particular, until his queries were answered.

———

"TWO DOUBLE EAGLES AND NO HAGGLING," E.J. said in a surprised tone, "I might have even asked fifty and got it."

In the office of the stable, she spoke to Cope as he set his rifle and gear in a corner of the room.

"Reckon he wanted the horse and had the wherewithal," Cope said, rather absently.

His weariness showed. Nearly a month on the trail, running down mustangs and hassling them back to town took its toll. The need for a hot meal and a bath overshadowed his attention span. He only half listened to his wife. Not readily noticing this, she replied.

"Well, he did seem taken by her. Still, there's something about him. Something doesn't sit right. Nothing he said or did. Fact is, he went out of his way to be mannerly and all. But, I don't know, something's just not right about him."

About that time, Cope realized that his wife had been without company for the duration of his trip and should have some notice paid to her. He turned from the wall and took her in his arms.

"Not exactly good timing," he said softly, "me smelling like I do, but I did miss you."

Before she could reply, he kissed her. His weeklong growth of beard was scratchy to her, but it was a small price to pay for this closeness which she also craved.

"I missed you, too."

He folded her into an embrace that enveloped her. She melted into it and remained there.

"I can deal with the smell," she said. "As long as it's yours."

He chuckled at that and squeezed her gently, then let her go.

"I better get cleaned up."

"I thought you were going to deliver that string."

"It's late and I'm tired. Tomorrow'll do. 'Sides, you're better looking than any of them horses."

"Thanks a bunch!"

He started for the door, smiling.

"So, what do you think?" she asked.

"About what?"

"That fellow. The buyer."

"What I think is he wanted the horse and didn't question the price. Why are you so interested? I'm the one that wore the badge, not you."

"I really think there's something off about him."

"What's this *hombre's* name?"

"Cholla, as I recall."

"All right, I'll go tell Rud to arrest Cholla."

She made a face at his absurd comment and chastised him, "Damn you, Cope. Go get cleaned up."

Their evening meal was taken at the cantina after Cope had bathed and both had changed into more presentable clothing. Wearing one of the very few dresses she owned, E.J. was a vision in powder blue. Cope proudly escorted her into the cantina to a table offered them by the owner. Acting the perfect gentleman, Cope seated her and then sat across from her, dropping his hat on an unoccupied chair.

While their meal progressed, Cholla entered the place. To reach the bar, he needed to walk past their table. Immediately recognizing E.J., he approached.

"Ah, *Señora* Worley, good evening," he said gregariously.

Cope and E.J. both looked his way as he reached them.

"I apologize for interrupting your dinner, but I had to tell you how beautiful you look."

His smile was broad by now as he observed the startled looks on their faces. E.J. tried to force a smile and failed at it. She maintained her manners, however.

"Why, thank you, Mr. Cholla. May I introduce my husband, Cope?"

"A pleasure, Sir. I am Lorenzo Cholla, at your service."

"How do?" Cope said simply.

"I am well, Sir. Please excuse my interruption. I merely wanted to convey my compliments to your wife. Having done so, I am on my way. I wish you both a pleasant evening."

Cholla bowed to them as they both said a forced thank you. He moved on toward the bar. E.J., embarrassed, put her hands over her face. Cope watched Cholla until he reached the bar.

"See what I mean about him?" E.J. asked, looking up.

"Well, I can't dispute his taste in women," Cope replied. "But, I got to tell you, there is something about him…. "

"That you just can't put your finger on, right?"

"Yep."

———

FOR CHOLLA, THE CHAIR ACROSS THE street from the bank became almost a permanent location. His quest to determine the details of the Wells Fargo coach delivery a day earlier had caused him to stake out this vantage point again this day. He took the chance that the sheriff might become suspicious of his presence, but since he maintained quite an unassuming posture, he went completely unnoticed.

At the point of the bank's start of business, he also watched Cope Worley lead a string of eight horses from the stable, up the street and out of town. He even tipped his hat pleasantly to Cope as he passed. Cope responded in kind.

At just about the same time as the delivery had occurred, another Wells Fargo coach rolled into town from the opposite direction toward the bank. Again, Rud Tanner stepped out of his office and made his way to the bank to meet the conveyance. There were the same number of guards with the driver, although they were all different personnel. Tanner accompanied the guards into the bank and, in short order, they emerged carrying the strongbox which was deposited inside the coach. Quickly, the coach was turned around and headed up the street in the direction from which it had come.

Cholla noted that the strongbox had resided in the bank for just about twenty-four hours. The next step in his information gathering effort was to determine if this was an isolated situation or a continuing operation. To this end, and to avoid the tedious and dangerous procedure of constantly watching the bank, he decided to start making other acquaintances and engaging in seemingly idle conversations.

5

CLYDE DURESCO WON THE HAND. IT was his business to do so. He had been sitting in this game for almost four hours and had gone through several players in the interim, winning in almost every case. This current trio was becoming disconcerted at his prowess and had started grumbling a few hands earlier. No accusations, just displeasure at losing. He remained silent and continued to play, maintaining his poker face and making certain that his hands were in constant sight of his opponents.

This was child's play for Duresco. Of course, he cheated but his moves were so smooth that the casual player missed every one of them, as he continued to pull in almost every pot.

He was a pleasant looking fellow with a long, finely featured face and slicked down blond hair that was neatly trimmed. Dressed decently in a dark suit, he seemed unassuming enough, intentionally so. Having become somewhat of a fixture in this saloon and gambling hall for the past few months, he had engaged many of the Senado Pass residents in games of chance, most of whom came away the worse for wear.

Cholla entered the establishment and gravitated to the

bar, but not before giving Duresco the once-over. Not as naive as most citizens, Cholla picked out this individual as an experienced gambler and, from the bar, observed the man. As he nursed his drink, one of the players slapped his cards down on the table and abruptly left the game. Seizing the opportunity, Cholla moved quickly to the table.

"Gentlemen, may I sit in?"

Each replied, including Duresco, in the affirmative. Cholla occupied the chair and produced both gold coins and paper currency. He was dealt into the next hand.

During the game, Cholla engaged the other participants in conversation, explaining that he was new in town and wanted to learn as much as he could about the place to determine if he might stay on. While Duresco kept quiet, the others were helpful. He left the competition almost one hundred dollars poorer but with knowledge of the connection between the bank and the Wells Fargo coaches. The strongbox apparently contained a payroll being transported by Wells Fargo. Senado Pass happened to be a stop-off point in the run, requiring different field offices to be involved. Also, quite apparent to him was the fact that Duresco cheated, although he decided against acting on this belief at the present time, tucking the tidbit away for future reference.

———

BASING HIS TIMING ON INFORMATION GLEANED from the poker table conversation in which he had engaged, Cholla entered the bank a few minutes earlier than the appointed time for the next Wells Fargo arrival. His excuse for being there was to open an account. This he expected to last long enough for him to observe the mechanics of the operation from inside the bank. Having watched the delivery, he made up his mind that an attack during the delivery process should be ruled out. That much fire power in the hands of knowledgeable individuals would cause this to go south in a heartbeat. No, it would need to be carefully planned to occur after the funds had been secured. Before the procedure was completed, Cholla left the bank with his new passbook in hand. He was already planning.

Constructing a cursory scheme told him he needed four participants, including himself. While two cleaned out the vault, the others would keep the bank employees and any customers at bay. Already considering Billy Griff and Duresco as two of the members, he first needed to seek out a fourth candidate. As he idly walked the streets, deep in thought, that contender came into his view.

They called him Chunky. He was big and slovenly with a round, pudgy face and an overgrown beard. His clothes, an undershirt that once was white and nondescript trousers supported by ragged suspenders and covered by a leather apron, were grimy and stained with sweat and dirt. Laboring as a blacksmith's lackey, he did the heavier lifting and the bidding of the smithy and was thankful for the opportunity to do so. Since no one else offered him gainful work, he took the owner's abuse and insults and did what he was told and offered up "yes, sirs" and "no, sirs" where other men would protest.

This scene before him caused Cholla to stop and observe as the blacksmith took Chunky to task for dropping something. He told him in no uncertain terms to clean up the mess by the time the smith returned, or he would be fired. As his employer stepped away on an errand, Chunky stooped to pick up that which he had allowed to fall.

Pretending concern, Cholla approached the big man. "Why do you let him treat you that way?"

"Come again?" Chunky, squatting in the process of doing

the work, looked around. His voice was scratchy and an octave higher than seemed appropriate for his size.

"Why do you let that man treat you like he does?"

"He's my boss."

"That does not give him the right to treat you like a slave. You should not stand for it."

"I know, but if I say something, he'll fire me. And ain't nobody else in this town going to hire me. I know that for a fact."

Cholla stooped and aided in the clean-up. "Allow me to help you."

"You don't got to."

"I want to."

When the work was finished, Cholla turned to him. "If I could, I would hire you, without a doubt."

Chunky smiled broadly. "You would? Well, thanks, Mister."

"*De nada.* You know, I might have something you can help me with that would bring you a lot of money."

Chunky continued smiling, anticipating. "Really? What would I do?"

"Look, I do not want to get you in trouble with the blacksmith. Meet me in the saloon when you get off work? I will explain then."

"In the saloon? Sure, I can do that."

"*Bueno.* What is your name?"

"It's Creighton Bond. But you can call me Chunky. Everybody does 'cause I'm so big."

"Then Chunky it is. I am Lorenzo Cholla. Call me Cholla. I will see you later in the saloon."

"I'll be there."

Cholla smiled at his new acquaintance and continued his walk, confident that he now knew the identity of the fourth member of his team.

—

LATER THAT AFTERNOON, HE APPROACHED DURESCO who stood at the bar of the saloon during a break in a poker game.

"Bartender." Cholla dropped a coin on the bar. "A drink for my friend here."

Duresco looked at him in surprise. "Thanks, Mister."

The bartender filled Duresco's glass and took the payment.

"Join me?" Cholla moved toward a table in the far corner. Duresco picked up his glass and followed. They sat across from each other. He immediately leaned closer and spoke in a low voice. "You are good, *amigo,* but I know you cheated during our game."

Duresco immediately became belligerent. "What'd you say?"

"I said you are a cheat," Cholla replied. "If I was able to catch it, others will. You will soon be found out and will put yourself in danger."

"I don't know what the hell you're talking about." Duresco attempted to make his protest seem in earnest.

"Yes, you know, *amigo,* you know. Not everyone is as gullible as some in this town. And when you are found out, it will not go well for you."

"That's my business."

"Amigo, I have a proposition for you that will give you the opportunity to make a lot of money for very little work. It will allow you to get away from this life before it kills you."

"Why the hell do you care whether I live or die?"

Cholla chuckled and shrugged. "I do not care, *amigo.* I am simply looking for someone who can assist me. You seem to be a good candidate."

"What the hell are you talking about, anyway?"

"I will explain in detail later. For now, I will say only that the proceeds will make anyone involved rich."

Now, Duresco leaned toward him, interested. "All right keep talking."

"This is definitely not legal, I must tell you that."

"You think I care about legal? If I did, I wouldn't take the chances I take."

"Bueno. There exists in this town at certain times a lot of money for those who are willing to take it."

"How much money we talking about?"

"I do not have an exact figure, but it has to be in the thousands based on the precautions they take to protect it."

"Thousands, eh? I'm in."

"It will be dangerous."

"Been there before," Duresco said, throwing off all cautions.

"Bueno. This will involve precise planning. We will need two more to join us. I am working on that. Once we have four, we will hold up the bank after the arrival of the Wells Fargo coach. That is when the bank vault will have the most money. We will do this one job and scatter after we split the money, and we will never see each other again."

"When do we do it?"

"I will contact you when the time comes. Until then, continue your regular activities."

Duresco rose from his chair and leaned close. "I'll be ready."

———

"HOWDY, MISTER CHOLLA. I COME LIKE you said." Chunky Bond spoke these words as he presented himself in front of Cholla who was still seated at the same table he had occupied during his conversation with Duresco.

"Sit down, Chunky."

Taking his seat, Chunky listened to Cholla's presentation of his plans to rob the bank and his pitch to get Chunky enough money to quit his job and leave Senado Pass. Chunky's simple mind grasped the concept but he found himself unwilling to break the law. Cholla convinced him that the law never did anything for him and probably would go against him if he were to balk at his treatment by the blacksmith. Chunky gradually came around but still refused to hurt anyone. Cholla assured him that this would never come to pass. The mere show of force would negate the necessity for the use of force. Chunky agreed to keep himself ready to be called on when the time came.

For the fourth member of his band, Cholla waited until the next day, having been unable to locate Billy Griff after making a thorough search of the town. As he left the cantina after breakfast, the door to the jail opened. In the doorway, Billy appeared and, behind him, Rud Tanner. An abrupt shove by Tanner pushed Billy out to the street. Tanner, carrying Billy's gun belt, stepped close to the young man and said loudly, as he thrust the belt into Billy's chest, "Stay the hell out of trouble, you dumbass kid! Next time I run you in, you lose that piece for good!" Billy clutched at the belt. Tanner stood with hands on his hips and watched Billy walk away.

Cholla began casually following Billy, out of town and about a half mile into the countryside. Keeping to the bushes, he observed as Billy strapped on the holster belt and lifted the gun out. He opened the loading gate and proceeded to load the weapon from the supply of cartridges on the belt. From behind a small boulder he produced a few tin cans and set them in a row on the boulder. For the next few minutes, he took shots at the cans, honing his speed and accuracy, until he had exhausted his ammunition. At that point, Cholla stepped in behind Billy.

"You are very good, Billy."

Startled, Billy spun on him and leveled the gun.

"I was sure you would do that," Cholla said, "so I waited until the gun was empty."

"Oh, howdy, Mr. Cholla. What you doing out here?"

"Watching you. I am impressed."

"Aw, that ain't nothing."

Billy took the opportunity to brag. "I'd do even better, I went up against somebody like Clay Allison."

"*Sí*, I am certain of that. Listen, Billy, I wanted to talk to you because I have a proposition for you."

"Yeah?"

"One that can get you much money, if you are interested."

"Sure, I'm interested. I need to buy more shells."

"Oh, Billy, what I have in mind will buy you much more than bullets."

Now, Billy showed interest. "How much you talking?"

Again, Cholla held out the bait. "Thousands, *mi amigo*. Thousands of dollars, all for the taking."

"Shit, you'd have to stick up a bank to get that much money at one time."

"Indeed, yes. That is my intention."

"Stick up a bank? You serious?"

A look of disbelief crossed the other man's face.

"I am. The bank right here in Senado Pass."

"Shit, you can't do that."

"Not alone, I can't. But, with the help of you and two others, it can be done."

Billy studied Cholla for a long moment.

"You're serious, ain't you?"

"*Sí*, I never joke about money. Every few weeks, Wells Fargo delivers a strongbox to the bank. It remains in the bank overnight and is taken out by Wells Fargo the next day. We will hit the bank after the delivery but before the pickup, and get away with more money than you can dream of. Come to the *cantina* tonight at six. We will have some dinner and you will meet the others who will do this. I will explain exactly how this will be done."

Billy nodded. "All right. Sure, I'll be there."

"Good man," Cholla said as he turned away. "Until six then."

———

AT A FEW MINUTES PAST SIX that evening, the four improbable acquaintances assembled in the cantina and took a table tucked away in a corner. After ordering, Cholla led the discussion regarding his plans.

Entering a few minutes later, E.J. and Cope occupied a small table in the center of the establishment with Cope facing in the direction of the four conspirators.

"Looks like your Mr. Cholla found some friends."

E.J. craned her neck to look. "How's he *my* Mr. Cholla?"

"Well, he's sure as hell not *my* Mr. Cholla. 'Sides, you're the one sold him the horse. You know any of them he's with?"

"Cope, you gave up the badge, remember? You told me to drop it."

"Just curious. Know any of them?"

"The big one works for the blacksmith. The young one just hangs around and gets into trouble, to hear Rud tell it. I don't know the dandy. Why?"

"Like I said, just curious."

E.J. made a face. He smiled but continued to study the group as the waiter approached.

6

ON THE DAY OF THE NEXT Wells Fargo delivery, Tanner went through the same motions as before, as did the Wells Fargo guards. While this transpired, Cholla observed from a different location but still took in all the details. As the empty coach rolled out of town, Cholla made the rounds of his recruits, informing each to assemble in a predetermined alley the next morning at nine, bringing with them guns and horses as well as the readiness to carry out the plan.

As the bank opened for business the next morning, E.J. left the stable and walked the short distance to the bank building, entering together with several other customers. She joined the line at the teller's cage to wait her turn.

Having secured their horses at the far end of the alley, Cholla and his cohorts exited the alley and strode toward the bank. Entering quickly, they spread to different locations from which they could see the patrons and the employees. As instructed previously, Duresco threw the lock on the door. At Cholla's signal, each drew a pistol before the inhabitants noticed their presence or intention.

"This is a holdup!"

The words created chaos as customers turned toward them, immediately frightened. E.J. remained quiet but recognized Cholla and noted his perfect English. She also realized that he was definitely not alone.

"Stay in the line!" Cholla pointed his pistol to emphasize the point. He made a gesture with his head, a signal to Duresco to join him and to Billy and Chunky to move in to cover the customers. With Duresco, he moved into the vault area and collared the man he had observed during his previous visit as the one in charge. This man was forced to bag the loose money inside the vault while Cholla and Duresco picked up the strongbox. As they exited, Cholla struck the man on the head with his gun barrel and pushed him falling to the side, then grabbed the money bag.

Rejoining Billy and Chunky, they handed the box to Chunky. He lifted it to his shoulder with no effort at all. They backed toward the door while Duresco preceded them to unlock it. With their attention drawn to the door, they failed to notice the teller pulling a revolver from under the counter.

"Stop!" The man leveled the gun as he shouted.

In the direct line of fire, E.J. attempted to push the man and the woman she stood with out of the way. Cholla looked around and, taking in the scene, instinctively fired his Colt. At that instant, E.J. moved slightly. Meant for the teller, the bullet bit into E.J.'s upper back as she screamed in pain and was propelled into the woman in front of her. The image of Cholla seared into her as she fell. Both women collapsed on the floor as he fired again, hitting the teller squarely in the chest.

"Out!" Cholla's voice rose with alarm, "Go!"

The four men piled through the doorway and hurried up the street to the alley.

The sound of the shots caused Rud Tanner to bound from his office into the street as he spotted the quartet running into the alley. Lifting his gun, he ran to the bank as people spilled out onto the street shouting. He stopped only long enough to understand their words. Then he continued to the alley and into it as Cholla and the others galloped away. Ineffectively, he fired off two shots after them before returning to the bank.

Customers and townspeople milled around outside the building. Tanner pushed his way through them and entered, immediately seeing the results of the muffled shots that had pulled him from his office.

"E.J.?" he said as he closed the distance to the spot where the woman lay.

He recognized the clothes more than the person since she was in a face down position. Reaching her, he went to a knee and hesitantly tried to move her. Blood stained her back and when he rolled her to her side, she cried out in pain.

A grunt indicating his disgust issued from him as his stomach came into his throat.

"Get the doc!" he managed to shout over his shoulder at the crowd outside.

The woman E.J. had fallen against was scrambling to get out of the way. Tanner stepped over E.J.'s body so he could face her without moving her again. He returned to his knee.

"Lay still, E.J. We're getting the doctor."

"Cholla!" She forced the name out.

Her voice was hoarse and weak. He leaned in closer to hear her better. It was not clear to him if she knew who he was.

"It's Rud, E.J. Just lay still. Doc's coming."

"Cholla—shot me—Cholla."

Tanner realized her intention but only concerned himself at this point with trying to save her. He needed to calm her and help her conserve her strength.

"Don't talk. Don't say nothing. You got to—"

He stopped there as her body relaxed and her head rolled

forward. His hand went to her wrist to check for a sign of life that his heart told him was not there. She was dead. That was a fact, but he could not admit it. Then the realization hit him.

"Oh, God, no. Not her. No. No. No." By the time he reached the last word, he wiped tears away from his eyes. He had known Cope for so many years and never known him to be so happy, so content as he was with E.J.

"How am I going to tell him?" he muttered, not fully realizing that he had spoken the words and not just thought them.

He stared at E.J.'s limp form and sniffled back the emotions he never before experienced. The scene was interrupted by the arrival of the doctor.

"Don't waste your time, Doc. She's gone."

The doctor confirmed this, all the same, as Tanner continued to stare at E.J.'s body. He moved only when a bystander called to him from behind the teller's cage having found the dead teller and the wounded banker. Stepping back there, he confirmed that the teller was dead and that the banker was beginning to regain consciousness. A quick glance into the vault told him the robbery had been successful.

"Doc!" He rose from the man and started toward the door.

The sight of E.J. again stopped him cold. "Shit!"

He forced himself back into the game, stepping onto the boardwalk and into the crowd's questions.

"There's two dead and they cleaned out the vault," he said. "Get guns and horses and meet back here fast. We're going out after them."

———

AT FULL GALLOP, CHOLLA LED HIS band of outlaws into the countryside. Certain that the sheriff would come after them, most likely with a posse, he intended to quickly divide the proceeds and scatter the group. Having scouted an assembly location beforehand, he now headed there with all possible speed. Struggling to keep up with Cholla's white mare, the others pushed their horses hard. After almost fifteen minutes of sustained riding, they arrived at a dense forest of mesquite trees which quickly swallowed them into the widespread branches. Confident of their temporary security in this location, Cholla drew rein and dismounted. His companions grouped around him. Duresco and Billy Griff dismounted and took the strongbox from under Chunky's arm, allowing the big man to also get down.

The subject of the stolen money, however, was not on Chunky's mind. Upset, he approached Cholla.

"You said wouldn't no one get hurt," he pointed an accusing finger, "but you shot two of them folks. And one was a lady. You had no call to do that. That weren't right."

Cholla had to calm the big man down or this would go badly.

"Chunky, I didn't want to hurt them. I had no choice. The teller had a gun. You saw that, didn't you? I shot at him, but the woman got in the way. If I didn't shoot him, he might have gotten one of us. Believe me, Chunky, it grieves me that it happened, but I can't change it."

Duresco added his thoughts. "Cholla's right. That teller was aiming right at us. He'd a got one of us sure."

The additional voice of reason started changing Chunky's mind. "Well, I reckon—"

"Chunky, I'm not a killer," Cholla interrupted him. "I hate this as much as you do. But I really had no other choice. If I could take back those bullets, I would."

"I reckon you're right." Chunky slowly nodded.

"When you take a chance at big stakes like this, sometimes you have to do some things you can't plan for."

"I reckon."

Cholla seized on the opportunity to change the subject.

"We need to divide this money and get away from here." He pulled the bag containing the loose money from his saddle and placed it near the strongbox. "Chunky, can you break this open?"

Chunky looked at the object and then stooped to lift a rock the size of the box. After dropping it on the box several times, the metal caved in and one of the hinges sprung. Standing the box on end, he dropped the stone once more, destroying the second hinge. Then he used his hands to pry the lid off while the lock remained intact, allowing access to the contents.

Cholla mingled the coins in the bag with the paper money and began counting. "Thirty thousand a hundred and forty." He spent a second or two ciphering. "That makes seventy-five hundred and thirty-five each."

"Not bad," Duresco said, grinning.

Cholla continued to count out four equal piles. Picking up his own, he rose and gestured to them to take theirs. When they had done this, he gave his last instruction. "Now scatter, everyone in a different direction. Get out of these parts and stay away. That sheriff will be looking hard for us. Wherever you go, keep your heads down. Don't flash that money around and don't attract attention. Find a new place and stay out of trouble. Go about your business like nothing ever happened. Stay down for six months to a year. Now mount up and get going."

Duresco and Billy, having completely understood Cholla's admonishment, went directly to their horses, mounted and rode out.

Chunky, however, hesitated. "I don't know where to go. I ain't never been no place but Senado Pass."

Cholla's own safety was dependent, in part, on Chunky's ability to stay hidden. He gave the big man further assistance.

"I know it's scary for you, Chunky, but you're your own man now. You're not beholden to any man. You can go and come as you like without anyone's say-so. And you can pay your own way. My advice is to head north or west. Try to get work, something you know how to do and settle down somewhere peaceful. You'll be fine."

"You really think so?"

"I do. As long as you don't spend that money like a soldier on a bender, you'll do fine."

"Well, all right, Mr. Cholla, if'n you say so."

Smiling proudly, Chunky moved slowly to his horse and mounted. "I'm going to head north."

He turned his horse in that direction.

Cholla watched him go before mounting and directing the white mare off to the northwest.

———

COPE ENTERED THE MAIN STREET OF Senado Pass hauling a string of ten mustangs, all prime examples of the breed. Weary from several days in the field, he led the horses around the stable and to the corral gate. He looked forward to a bath and a hot meal, as well as at least a kiss and a hug from E.J., but he had to get these animals into the corral first. Later, he could separate them into stalls and care for them. Right now, the corral would retain them and allow him to become human again. Opening the gate, he shooed them in and quickly secured them. Then he dismounted and tied off his horse.

Entering the stable interior, he called out to announce his presence. "E.J., I'm back."

Strangely, there was no response. As he walked past its stall, he noted that E.J.'s horse was there. He moved to the office.

"E.J., you here?"

The room was empty, and it looked to have been that way for a time. Where was she? It's not mealtime. She's usually here.

Just to convince himself that she was not, he called her name again. The reply surprised him.

"Cope."

The voice was not E.J.'s. It was Rud's. He turned at the sound to see Tanner standing in the doorway. The expression on his friend's face foretold bad news. Tanner had that kind of face. His moods could be easily read.

"Rud, you seen E.J.? She should be here."

"Cope," Tanner said again but failed to continue.

"What's wrong?" Cope asked. Something was coming.

Tanner sucked in a breath and let it out loudly.

"Cope, there ain't no fitting way to tell you this but straight out. E.J.'s ... Aww, Cope, E.J.'s dead."

The full meaning of Tanner's words failed to make it to his brain. Maybe he's playing some kind of sick joke. But that was not Tanner's way, especially not with a subject as grave as this.

"What?" Cope asked, as if he had not heard correctly.

Tanner took a step closer. His hand went out as if to touch his friend—but it just stayed out there.

"Cope, I'm so sorry. E.J. ... is dead."

Cope just looked at the man. It can't be. How can she be dead? It can't be.

"Can't be," he said, mimicking his thought, shaking his head.

Tanner moved closer. Now, the hand went to Cope's shoulder to sort of symbolically shore up his friend. In reality, he was steadying himself to continue this.

"It is, Cope. I wished it wasn't, but it is. She's gone."

Now the realization took hold. Cope's face scrunched up first in disbelief and then in grief. The weight of it caused him to lean back against the desk for support.

"Where is she?" he asked lucidly, after a moment of contemplation.

"At the doc's."

"I got to see her."

The need to see the body of his wife became suddenly of vital importance. Whether to convince himself that it was true or that he just had to see her one last time was unclear to him. In fact, nothing about this made any sense. He had to see her. Brushing past Tanner, he hurried out to the street and went at a trot toward the doctor's office. Tanner fell in behind and followed.

Bursting into the office, Cope stopped short as the doctor turned. "E.J."

Nothing more would come out.

Recognizing him, the doctor indicated a door to his right. Cope went in. Tanner entered the office at that point and the doctor's hand halted him. He waited.

E.J.'s body lay on a table covered completely by a white sheet. Cope peeled back the sheet to reveal her expressionless face. No smile. Not like E.J. But there's no expression in death, and she was indeed dead. E.J. was dead. His lovely E.J.—the best part of him—dead. She was no more. And now he was sure of it.

Tears welled up in his eyes and rolled down his cheeks as the realization gripped him. Staring at her, he held back the hysterics that were trying to break free for he could not allow that. He had to be in control. He had to. For her sake, he had to stay in command of his emotions. This had to be seen through.

"Cope."

Tanner stood behind him, and now the training and instincts Cope had developed as a lawman took hold. He wiped away the tears with the back of his hand.

"When?" he asked almost clinically.

"Two days back."

"How?"

"Shot. She was in the bank when it was robbed. They tell me she got in the way of a bullet meant for the teller. It got her in the back."

"Who?"

"They say it was some hombre name of Cholla."

"Cholla," he said through gritted teeth.

"I'll get him, Cope. I've had a posse out tracking them since it happened."

Now Tanner rambled some, attempting to reassure Cope and somehow experiencing responsibility for this entire situation. "We done found where they stopped to open the strongbox. Hell, they mangled the shit out of that thing," he said. "We going out again in the morning. Just a matter of time. I'll run that Cholla down, sure."

"No," Cope said shortly, resolutely. "He's mine—I've got a crow to pluck."

——

E.J.'S FUNERAL WAS HELD A DAY later. By now, numb with grief, Cope went through the motions. Few people attended because few people knew them. Tanner elected to continue the search for the fugitives, so he was absent. Truth be told, he was unable to endure the ritual. He expressed his sincere thoughts to Cope beforehand and used the chase as an excuse.

The grave and headstone were simple, displaying only her full name and her nickname, the dates of her birth and death. Cope stood at the gravesite long after the attendees left. He talked to E.J., talked to her as if she was still with him for he had not yet wrapped his mind around the fact that his beloved was gone. Only when Tanner returned from his search late that afternoon and came to the cemetery did Cope react to outside stimulus.

"Cope," Tanner said as he approached, "you likely been standing here since morning. This ain't good."

"She's gone, Rud." Cope said flatly, "I can't see her. I can't hear her."

"Cope, she wouldn't want you to be like this. She thunk too much of you. I know that for a fact. She'd want you to move on."

He turned suddenly on Tanner, rage in his eyes and on his face. "How? How do you move on from this? She said she didn't want to have to bury me. Now I—There's only two things I can think of right now. She's gone—and Cholla."

"Don't you worry none about Cholla. I'll make him pay. You go ahead on and get on with your life."

"What life?"

He brushed past Tanner and walked away slowly. The sheriff looked after him, then back to the grave. He shook his head in futility.

few times in Senado Pass, but darkness made the identity more difficult. Needing certainty, he slipped off the barrel and walked toward the wagon as the driver climbed down off the seat. Using his floppy hat to beat the dust from his clothing, the newcomer's back was turned as Cope approached.

"Don't move." He shouldered the shotgun. "Stay right where you are."

"You talking to me?"

"I'm talking to you. There's a shotgun trained on your back. See you do as I say, and it won't go off."

"I don't want to get shot none."

"Raise your hands and turn around."

The big man did as instructed. As he turned, the pistol secured in his waistband showed. As a precaution, Cope stepped into an aggressive stance behind the shotgun. The light from behind him lit the other man's face.

Chunky Bond. It was him, all right.

"Reach that pistol out with two fingers and hold it out where I can see it."

Chunky readily obeyed, extracting the weapon from his waistband and holding it away from his body.

"Let it fall." Chunky opened his fingers and let the handgun drop to the ground. "Now head for the stable back there. See you do nothing but walk and do it slow."

He motioned with the shotgun to start Chunky's movement. Staying a safe distance behind, he walked his prisoner to the stable. As they entered, he continued giving orders. "Get that rope off my saddle there and loop it around your wrist."

Chunky did as he was told.

"Face the saddle."

The man complied, turning his back. Standing the shotgun against the cask, Cope picked up the rope and, pulling Chunky's other hand behind the man's back, secured both wrists together.

Then recovering the gun, he kept it at hip level, trained on Chunky's back.

"Mister, why you doing this? I ain't done nothing to you."

"Your name's Bond. Chunky Bond."

"Y—yeah?" The answer was guarded. He was uncertain of how this man knew his name.

"You're known to be one of the *hombres* that robbed the bank in Senado Pass and killed two people in the doing."

"Oh, I didn't kill nobody, mister. I done what you said, but I didn't kill nobody. I wouldn't do nothing like that."

"One of them killed was my wife."

"I'm sorry. I didn't mean for nobody to get hurt. I told him that when I signed on. We just take the money and go, I says. But it went bad. He didn't have no choice but to shoot. He was protecting us."

"Who's *he?*"

"Mr. Cholla. He was protecting us. He didn't want to shoot, but he had to."

"Where's this Cholla now?"

"I don't know, mister. We all split up after we got our shares. Billy and Mr. Duresco, they headed north, I think. And Mr. Cholla, I think he was heading northwest, last I seen of him. And I come here. That's all I know."

"Where's your share?"

"In my poke over to the warehouse. I been staying there since I got here. You a lawman, mister?"

"I was once. No more. I want Cholla. Where is he?"

"I done told you I don't know where he's at. Mister, what's going to become of me?" Chunky asked fearfully.

"You'll likely hang."

"But I didn't kill nobody. You got to believe me."

"Law says anyone involved is as guilty as the one pulls the trigger. That means you'll hang."

"Please, mister, don't hang me. I didn't mean for none of this to happen. I'm sure sorry about your wife."

"Hanging's up to the law, not me. I'm taking you in is all. You'll get more of a chance than my wife got. You'd best shut your mouth now and do what I tell you."

He complied. Cope walked him back to the warehouse and to his bunk inside to retrieve the bank money, then back to the stable to wait while he saddled his horse. He pressed the bareback packhorse into service for Chunky to ride.

"Where we going, mister?" Apparently, the fat boy forgot the order to shut his mouth, "Where you taking me?"

"To the closest town that's got law. You can beg them for mercy all you got a mind to. Won't work on me."

Surprised at the ease with which he was able to take Chunky down, and almost sorry for the big man for being so easily led into this mess, Cope moved his prisoner to an established town nearby. Acting like the lawman he once was, he called on the local town marshal and turned Chunky and the recovered loot over to the law. He asked that the prisoner and the money be returned to the custody of Rud Tanner. The marshal, upon seeing the wanted poster, agreed to take care of the situation and Cope trusted that it would be done.

Returning to Castle Wells to pick up his belongings, he remembered what Chunky had said as to the disposition of the other fugitives. Needing more specifics to be able to locate his targets, he flipped a coin to decide which direction he would take. Heads, it would be north. Tails, northwest.

The coin landed heads up.

He rode north in search of either Billy Griff or Clyde Duresco. Maybe one of them could lead him to Cholla.

THE
CHEROKEE
OUTLET

8

STRIKING OUT FROM THE MESQUITE GROVE on the day of the robbery, Clyde Duresco and Billy Griff rode together, heading north. Not exactly compatible, they endured each other for mutual protection and safety on the trail. Their only common thread was the fact that both were glad to be shed of the liability of Chunky Bond and his conscience. Neither could be less concerned with the killing of the teller and the woman. As long as they had money in their pockets, nothing else mattered.

Repeatedly, Duresco tried to entice Billy into a card game, holding out the possibility of doubling his gains. But Billy was too smart to be suckered into any game with Duresco. Fed up with the constant prodding, he threatened Duresco with gunplay if he failed to back off. Duresco, cognizant of Billy's prowess with a gun, quit his overtures. Thereafter, the balance of their trip passed in silence throughout the northern trek through Texas. As they approached the extension of the Indian Territory known as the Cherokee Outlet, the uneasy alliance reached its end.

"Yonder's where I'm headed," Billy pointed. "Cherokee

Outlet they calls it. Full of every outlaw and runaway you can think of. Ain't no lawman looking to stay alive'll go in there."

Duresco smiled. "Sounds like your kind of people, Billy, not mine. I need the yokels, the trusting souls, them that can't talk to you and watch your hands at the same time. I hear Kansas is north of here. Always wanted to run a game in Dodge. Lot of money in that town."

"Suit yourself." Billy headed northwest into the territory.

"Yeah," Duresco said, "you, too."

Duresco continued riding north toward Kansas.

———

BILLY'S RIDE INTO THE OUTLET WAS short, less than a day beyond the border. There he came upon a settlement. He noticed several riders stationed nearby carrying rifles. The sign on the side of the road identified it as Lautertown. But, infinitely more threatening than the name, the caveat under it stated, *Enter at Your Own Risk.* Far from being put off by the statement, Billy became instead interested, even intrigued. Having stopped to read the sign, he now continued up the trail toward the first of several buildings visible beyond the marker.

Raucous activity met him as he rode slowly into the town. Men dressed in dusty trail clothes moved about. Very few women were visible on the street, but high-pitched female laughter came from more than one saloon and gambling hall lining the main street. Billy continued his ride until his notice crossed the sign over a particularly well kept and well positioned building. It drew his attention and caused him to pull rein at the crowded hitch rail outside. Before dismounting, he studied the wording above the swinging doors. *Lauter's Den, Emmett Lauter, prop.* Maybe this fellow, Lauter, was the one to see.

The sounds coming from within portrayed this as a

popular hangout. He stepped down and tied off. He flipped the saddlebags across his shoulder, mounted the boardwalk in front of the establishment, hiked up his pants and gun belt to enhance his appearance and stepped inside.

Immediately, the mangled speech and laughter of men unconcerned with their behavior and the screams and giggles of scantily dressed women, encouraging these men to spend their money on drinks and other, more personal pastimes, assaulted his ears. There were none of the controls brought to bear on this activity that had been the norm in Senado Pass and other towns Billy had visited. Here there was an openness and an acceptance, even promotion, of these practices. Quickly, Billy liked this place, at least initially.

As he moved toward the bar, a scene played out in front of him. Two men already at the bar stepped back from each other, obviously at odds. Quick movements were carried out by both, but one was faster. Gunfire resounded in the barroom, resulting in one of the men crumpling against the bar, his weapon discharging aimlessly into the floor. The victor displayed his gun to the crowd as they backed away. Billy stopped and tried to shake the deafness from his ears that was the result of the close quarters of the shots. Some of it dissipated, enough for him to hear slightly, as the man with the gun became the only one left at the bar. As the gun smoke rose lazily toward the ceiling, the other occupants stepped further away.

"You got one chance to drop that and pay up," a deep, gruff voice shouted from Billy's left, "or you're a dead man."

At a door on the left, a short, stocky man with a square, resolute face and thinning hair stood. Sporting a thin, well-manicured mustache and clad in expensive dress clothing, this man presented an authoritative figure. The conversion revolver in his hand added to his appearance of power.

"And now there's the matter of my enforcer's demise.

That'll cost you a hundred more," he said, "That's a hundred and fifty total. Cough it up."

Billy watched as the gunman turned to face the well-dressed man. Both leveled their weapons on the other but the well-dressed man's gun was already cocked, giving him a slight edge. Apparently gauging his chances in this as less than good, the gunman allowed his pistol to slip from his hand and drop to the floor. The other man continued covering his target.

"Now the money."

The gunman reached inside his vest at the command, giving the impression of obedience. But the quick movement he made next did not produce money. From his vantage point, Billy caught the move sooner and reacted faster. He had no clue why he did so, save for the fleeting thought that the well-dressed man somehow seemed more important to him than the gunman. Observing a Derringer swinging out from inside the vest, Billy pulled his own piece and fired, almost automatically. Before the little gun could be cocked, Billy's bullet entered the man's side, high enough to rip through vital organs. It slammed him into the bar and, as he dropped the pistol, he folded in a heap on the floor. Again, the loudness of the small explosion interrupted hearing.

Billy stood transfixed by the gravity of his deed. He had drawn and fired his weapon many times before, but this was the first time he had ever actually shot anyone with it. The numbness in his brain cleared away slightly when the well-dressed man approached him and spoke.

"That was pretty fast, kid."

Only half aware of the words, they broke Billy's trance enough to make him turn toward the voice.

"What? Oh, yeah, I reckon—"

"You can put that away now. He's down."

Slowly, Billy holstered his gun.

"What's your name, kid?"

Billy began slowly returning to full functionality. "Name's Billy Griff."

"I'm Emmett Lauter. I own this place and the rest of the town. You just done me a good turn, Billy. I won't forget it. That ranny owed me money. Go take it off him. It's yours now."

"How much?"

"Take all he's got. He won't no more need it."

Billy moved forward and stopped at his victim. Without concern for the man's condition, he crouched and rifled through the clothing, trying to avoid the blood, and finding considerably more than the amount Lauter had mentioned. Quickly, he pocketed the funds and got up. Lauter came to his side.

"Barney," Lauter said to the bartender who still cowered with the crowd, "come here and set them up."

Reluctantly, the barkeep returned to his duties, placing two glasses in front of them. He filled them from a bottle labeled Kentucky Bourbon. Lauter picked up both glasses and handed one to Billy.

"Bottoms up." He tossed his drink down.

Billy followed suit, finding the liquor smoother than any of the rotgut he had, up to now, experienced. He smiled.

Lauter leaned against the bar. "You know, Billy, I can use a man like you. See, I run this town as a hideout for men running from the law. For a price, they can stay here as long as they want. Or as long as they can afford to and cause no trouble. And, to make sure they pay up or get out, I need an enforcer. Creel, there, he didn't last very long. The job's yours if you want it. Your room and board and your meals are free, and I'll give you ten percent of everything you collect. If they don't pay up, well, you just proved you can handle that. What do you say?"

Billy grinned. This was a windfall. Not only could he make

more money, but he would have the opportunity to prove his worth as a gunfighter. A winning situation.

"You got yourself a *in forcer.*"

They shook hands on the agreement.

———

HAVING RIDDEN DUE NORTH FROM CASTLE Wells, Cope made frequent stops in towns and villages he came across. His stays were brief, however, allowing time only to replenish supplies and to question every person with whom he came in contact. The query was simple. He displayed the wanted poster and asked if they had seen any of those identified therein. More often than not, the answer was no. Some deviations occurred. A few thought they recognized one or more of the images but, upon deeper probing, he found them mistaken.

Not until he reached Abilene did his luck change. After stabling his horses, he made the rounds of the town, exhausting several of the saloons fairly quickly. By now, needing a drink, he entered the last of these establishments with no expectation of achieving much more than quenching his thirst.

As he approached the bar which lined the back wall of the building, he assessed the occupants. Drunks or casuals, likely no help from them. He ordered a beer and proceeded to interview them anyway. As expected, this prompted no new information, until he reached a buckskin clad man who, full of trail dust, seemed obviously fresh from travel. A big man, bigger than Cope in height and weight, and quite well developed. His black hair was profuse, having been neglected for what seemed like years. An unruly beard covered his long face. Nursing a beer alone at the end of the bar, he looked around as Cope slid in beside him.

"Got a minute, friend?"

"Reckon so. Long as it don't cost me nothing." His voice

as deep as his size, it had a smooth quality that seemed cordial enough, if not exactly friendly.

"Nothing but time and not much of that," Cope said.

The man turned to face him. "What's on your mind?"

He slipped the poster from his shirt pocket and opened it out on the bar. "I'm looking for these men. Wondering if you seen any of them."

The man studied the images. "You a lawman?"

"Nope."

"Bounty hunter?"

"Nope."

"So, it's personal."

Cope nodded. "One of the people killed during that robbery was my wife."

"Hmm. Lost a couple of them myself. Ain't easy. Let's see...." Looking more carefully at the poster, he singled out Billy Griff and pointed to that likeness. "I seen him."

"Whereabouts?"

"So, I's coming back from a hunt up in Coloradi and I passed through the Cherokee Strip. Two weeks back it was. First time I done that. Usual go down through New Mexico Territory. Come upon a town, Lautertown it was called, as I recollect. Anyways, they's a bunch of no goods there and this one was some kind of a collector. He's taking money if'n you want to stay there, hideout from the law and the like. Nasty little shit, he was. I didn't want no part of that place so's I moves on. But that's him, I reckon. That's the damned kid I run into."

"You're sure that's him?"

"Sure am. He come as close as you to me 'fore I figured out I ought to get away from him and get shed of that place right fast."

"How do I get to this Lautertown?"

"Just head northwest out of Abilene past Amarillo. Soon's you get to the border, the other side, you can see it in the distance. You oughtn't go there though. That kid'll kill you soon as look at you. I seen it in his eyes. Cold eyes he had. Look straight through you."

"I'll take my chances." He folded and pocketed the poster. "Thanks for your telling. Can I buy you a drink?"

"Save your money, stranger. You go up there, you'll surely need it."

———

AFTER CONSULTING WITH THE MAN ABOUT trail conditions, Cope set out immediately for the Cherokee Outlet border. Figure it to be about three hundred odd miles. Press the horses to make better than twenty miles a day, should get to Lautertown in a little more than two weeks. Stopping only to eat and sleep sparingly, he pressed on and came within sight of the town on the fourteenth day.

By this time, not having shaved since arriving in Castle Wells, Cope's face was covered in a full beard, making him almost unrecognizable. Should help me play the ruse I'm planning.

As he approached, the sentries watching the road came into view. Remember that for future reference. He continued past the town signpost and on into the main street. Moving slowly, wearily, he proceeded to the hitch rail outside Lauter's Den. This Lauter *hombre* looked to be the one in charge.

He dismounted. Before entering the building, he spent a long moment securing the horses' reins, during which he committed to memory an overview of the street on which he stood. Might be useful if a quick exit is needed. Keep that picture in mind.

He stepped inside the establishment and moved with a slow swagger to the bar. His preference was immediately requested by the bartender to which he replied, "Whiskey."

The payment demand accompanied delivery of the product. "Two bits."

Cope fished out a shiny, twenty-dollar gold piece and dropped it on the bar noisily. That should attract attention. "Leave the bottle."

The bartender set the bottle down and moved away. Cope finished the glassful and poured another. As he did so, the door to Lauter's office opened and Lauter stepped out to observe the new arrival. His hands pushed back his jacket and rested on his hips as he downed his second drink and poured a third.

Arms at his sides, Lauter stepped quickly to Cope's location. "Howdy, stranger. Just get into town?"

He fingered the glass without turning. "Yep."

"Planning on staying?"

"What's it to you, I stay or go?"

"I'm figuring you're running from something from the look of you. And, if you're looking to hole up a spell, I can provide that for a price."

Cope wheeled. "What makes you think I'm on the run?"

"Been on the trail better than a week, I'd say. Likely going day and night. Not many'll do that 'less they're trying to put distance 'tween them and something—or someone."

"Say you're right. What do you get if I stay?"

"Fifty a week. That'll get you the run of the town and protection from the law. You can enjoy that for as long as you keep paying and keep your ass out of trouble."

"And, if I don't?"

From behind him, Cope's question was answered sharply by a third, younger voice, "Then you deal with me."

9

BILLY GRIFF STOOD WITH HIS HAND hovering over the butt of his holstered weapon. Cope turned slowly toward the sound of the new voice to see the young man pictured on the poster.

Billy didn't recognize him—exactly how he had hoped this might play out. But this was just the beginning. Much more to accomplish before this ended.

Cope raised his hands to slightly above his hips, palms out, displaying acquiescence. "Ain't looking for trouble, just a place to light."

"Then pay the man and we're done."

Needing time to work out how exactly to wear his prey down, he reached carefully into his pocket to produce the required funds. Without taking his eyes off Billy, he handed the money to Lauter.

"That buys you a week from right now, stranger." Lauter pocketed the money. "By the way, what do they call you?"

"Stranger'll do. I'm buying a place to stay, no questions asked."

Lauter grinned. "Fair enough… Stranger." He turned on his heel and walked away.

Cope's glance returned to Billy. "Relax, kid. You look a tad jumpy to me. Have a drink."

"I'm just fine, Mister."

He shrugged and tossed back the rest of the whiskey, wiping his mouth with the back of his hand. "Suit yourself."

He started for the door.

Billy's gaze followed. "Hey! I'll see you in a week."

"Or sooner." Cope kept walking. He needed to keep the kid off balance.

By the end of the day, he'd stabled his horses and secured a room at one of the hotels. After stowing his gear, he took to the street to locate and observe his quarry. He made no secret of it. He wanted Billy to know he was being watched. The kid was too confident, too secure.

It was time to put him on the defensive.

Into the second day, Billy noticed the stranger lurking nearby. At first, he took no heed of this annoyance. But, little by little, the presence of this silent observer began making him nervous. He would approach one of the people from whom it was time to collect another fee and would see the stranger in the background. After completing the task, the stranger was nowhere to be seen. Then he would turn up at another encounter and similarly disappear. With each additional situation, Billy became more conscious of this and more upset with the intrusion.

While Cope did nothing more than watch, his being there accomplished his purpose. Billy acted increasingly more nervous with his shakedown victims, almost to the point of losing the upper hand. Determined to put an end to this, Billy sought the stranger out. Gauging this from the kid's body language, Cope made himself scarce, giving Billy a false sense of conclusion. Then, less than a day later, Cope appeared again.

Now completely unnerved, Billy brushed past his latest mark and stormed toward him. "Something you want, stranger?"

Leaning against a building, Cope pushed his hat onto the back of his head. "Why? Am I making you jumpy, kid?"

Billy just became more agitated. "You been tailing me for days now, watching me. What the hell do you want?"

"Nothing."

"Then quit following me!"

"Why? Does that make you nervous?"

"Shut up! Just stay away from me!" Billy assumed the stance of a gunfighter ready to draw.

Cope lifted his hat and placed it back on his head in the correct position, then pushed off from the building and walked slowly away. "Reckon I do make you jumpy some."

Fuming, Billy stamped his foot in the dirt. "Hey! Turn around! I'm still talking to you!"

"I'll keep going, kid," Cope said over his shoulder. "Don't want to make you any more jumpy."

"You son of a bitch!"

"Calm down. No need to get riled."

Cope kept moving as Billy, now fit to be tied, just stood there. Stifling the urge to shoot this bastard because Lauter would have his hide for eliminating a paying customer, his fists clenched tightly as he watched Cope slowly walk away.

No contact between the two occurred again for two days. During that time, Billy settled down and returned to performing his duties adequately. Then Cope reappeared. He watched and disappeared by the time Billy's collections were finished. After three of these incidents, Billy decided to bring this to an end. He neglected his next collection and waited for Cope to show up. At first sight, Billy hurried into an alley that allowed him to return to the street behind Cope. He drew his gun and poked it into Cope's back.

"This ends now!" he said into Cope's ear. "Get into that alley or I'll cut you in half right here."

Cope raised his hands to just below his shoulders to display compliance. He moved as instructed into the alleyway in front of him. Billy followed closely, never removing the gun barrel from its threatening location.

"I think that's far enough," Billy said as they reached halfway into the tight corridor.

Cope stopped.

"Now, I want to know why you're shadowing me!"

"You," Cope said. "You're the reason I'm here."

"What the hell's that supposed to mean? Come on, out with it!"

"I come to take you back, kid."

Cope chose his words carefully. That should unnerve Billy and distract him as well.

"Back where?" Billy said, taking the bait. "You better tell me the whole of it."

"Back to Senado Pass, Billy. You're wanted there. Robbery and murder, Billy. Robbery and murder. That's why I'm here."

"You some kind of lawman, stranger? All I got to do is tell Lauter about you and you won't last a minute."

"Robbery and murder, Billy."

"I didn't kill them two!"

That got him. Push harder. "Maybe you didn't pull the trigger, Billy, but you being there makes you just as guilty as Cholla."

"How do you know about Cholla?"

"I know about a lot of things, Billy. I know the law'll hang you just as quick as they'll hang Cholla. And I know the woman that was killed in the bank that day. She was my wife, Billy, and you took her from me, you and Cholla and the rest of them. That's why I'm here, kid. Because of her, because of my wife."

"I didn't kill her. Cholla done it. It was him done it."

Billy, now engulfed in his protest, allowed his attention to shift to that and away from covering Cope. That's where I want him. The gun barrel moved away from his back. Cope spun to his left and dropped his left hand, sweeping it in front of him as he turned. The hand hit the gun barrel and kept going, pushing the weapon to Billy's right and away from Cope's body. At the same time, his right hand came across Billy's face, forcefully delivering a slap that shifted Billy's weight and opened a cut at the corner of his mouth. Without a pause, Cope reversed his right hand, now clenched in a fist and connected with Billy's nose. The force of the blow pitched Billy backwards and off balance. Cope's left hand grabbed Billy's right wrist to immobilize the gun while his right fist snapped forward to connect with Billy's mouth. Billy sagged as Cope let go of his gun hand to allow him to fall to the ground. Immediately, Cope's boot stomped down on Billy's wrist, causing him to release the pistol.

Through clouded vision, Billy watched Cope's gun come out and level on him.

"Now, you stupid son of a bitch," Cope said, "get up!"

Sniveling from his wounds, Billy got his feet under him and hauled himself up.

"Pick up your gun and unload it."

Billy stooped and lifted the gun off the ground. Cope looked at him. He's thinking about using it. Cope cocked his own weapon.

"Don't try it, kid. Just unload it."

The young outlaw went through the unloading procedure, allowing the five cartridges to drop to the ground.

Cope lowered the hammer of his gun to half cock and turned the cylinder to relocate the empty chamber under the hammer. Then he closed the hammer on the empty chamber. "Holster it."

Billy obeyed and then issued a warning of his own. "You ain't making it out of this town taking me with you. The guards'll stop you."

"I'll worry about that. Where's your share of the bank money?"

"The hell with you!"

Cope shifted his gun to his left hand and used his right hand to deliver a cross to the kid's jaw. The blow ripped his head to the side and slammed him against the building wall, shaking his insides.

He placed the revolver barrel inches from Billy's head and spoke through gritted teeth. "I'm no more a lawman, Billy, so I'm not bound by rules. You tell me what I ask you or you won't like what comes next."

Billy now understood that with which he dealt and rethought his defiance. He rubbed the bruise on his jaw. "It's in my hotel room."

"Take me to it."

Billy pulled himself upright and started toward the street with Cope following closely. Although Cope holstered his gun, he remained ready to react to any false move the kid might concoct. But Billy bided his time and carried out the order, waiting for the right moment to turn the tables on his adversary. He led the way to the hotel room and dutifully produced the bank loot which Cope stashed inside his shirt, then waved his pistol in the direction of the door.

"Head for Lauter's place."

———

EMMETT LAUTER, SEATED AT HIS DESK, responded to the knock on his office door. "Who's out there?"

"It's Billy. I got to talk to you."

"Come on in."

The door opened and Lauter paid little attention to it. Billy appeared in the doorway and, a split second later, was propelled into the room by Cope's shove. Quickly, Cope stepped in and closed the door.

Startled, Lauter looked up to see his enforcer stumbling away from the desk after being stopped by it. Cope stood at the door with his pistol drawn and ready.

Lauter's brow rose. "What the hell is this?"

Billy began apologizing but Cope spoke over him, cutting him off. "Stay where you are, Lauter. Stay right there."

"What do you want?"

"I'm taking Billy out of here and you're going to help me." Cope waved the barrel of his revolver between the two men. "I'll shoot the first one of you that tries anything. Am I clear?"

Lauter, trying to buy time, turned his attention to Billy. "How'd you let this happen?"

Billy, still nursing his facial wounds, stuttered out an answer. "He—he got the drop on me."

Cope took a long step closer. "There's no discussion here. Shut up and do what I tell you."

"All right, stranger," Lauter said. "You're holding the cards."

"Stand up. Drop your gun belt."

Lauter stood slowly, carefully, and unbuckled his holster belt. He allowed the rig to drop to the floor.

"Kick it away."

He did so. It slid off to his right, close to Cope.

Cope kicked it further toward the wall. "We're going to ride out of town and you're going to keep your guards away."

"We'll need horses to do that."

"We'll get horses." He straightened his arm, sticking the barrel of his gun under the other man's nose. "Just remember one thing—if this goes bad, I'll drop you both before I go down. I got nothing to lose."

Certain they were convinced of his determination, Cope marched the pair to the stable and ordered them to saddle his mount, along with two others. Then he had them prepare his packhorse.

The kid attempted to leave the strap on Cope's saddle loose enough to cause it to slip.

Cope shook his head. "Tighten up that cinch."

Billy complied.

He directed them into their saddles. "Lead the way. Don't forget. I'll be right behind you—and so will my gun."

They rode out in the direction Cope had arrived from and kept the pace to little more than a walk.

"You know, stranger, lawmen don't last long in the strip," Lauter said.

"I'm not a lawman," Cope replied. "And I'll last as long as I need to—longer'n you will."

Their course brought them within close proximity of two guards on horseback. Spotting the trio, the guards turned their horses toward them and began riding fairly quickly in their direction.

"Keep riding." Cope holstered his weapon. "They stop us, you talk 'em down."

Lauter did not reply. The sentries came in close and drew rein. One of them recognized Lauter and greeted him, asking why they were there.

"We're just out for a ride, gents," Lauter replied.

Catching the man's attention, he made a gesture with his eyes toward Cope. Still behind them, Cope did not see this act. Lauter did not pursue it.

"Sure, Mr. Lauter," the guard said. "You go on and enjoy your ride."

"See you, boys." Lauter directed his horse forward. Billy joined him, and Cope brought up the rear as they walked their horses past the guards.

He fought the urge to look back until it was safe.

Proceeding along the trail, they followed it into a right-hand turn that afforded him the opportunity to glance back.

The two guards rode hard in a parallel course. Lauter must have somehow tipped them. Now they were riding to cut the trio off and ambush them.

"Whip them up, you two. Ride like hell."

Lauter dug his heels into his horse's flanks and slapped the reins across its rump, generating an immediate gallop. Billy followed suit. Cope got his mount up to the same speed as they rode up the trail. Keeping them in sight, Cope scanned the forward area for a place to hide. That outcropping of rocks on the left, with the rough trail leading to it.

That would do it.

"Go left." He had to shout to be heard. "Up that trail."

Lauter and Billy pulled their mounts left and headed up the narrow trail as Cope followed. "Pull up."

With his gun out and covering them, Cope corralled them into a rock grouping. They were forced to stop. With a sudden jerk, Lauter pulled his horse around and slammed it into Cope's mount. As the animals collided, Lauter attempted to launch himself from the saddle at Cope.

But Cope, having let go of the packhorse, was able to control his mount. As Lauter leapt forward, he swung his revolver and caught the man in the temple with the barrel. Lauter went limp and dropped between the two horses. Cope pulled his horse back, but Lauter was already under the hooves of his own horse which had panicked at the activity. Lauter's body sustained several telling blows delivered by the hooves as the horse flailed around.

While this happened, Billy directed his horse away from the fracas and pulled his gun from his holster. Hastily attempting to feed cartridges from his belt into the weapon, the unsteadiness of the animal caused him to drop several. He tried again. That gave Cope enough time to recover and to level his own weapon on Billy.

"Drop it!"

Billy hesitated, one bullet in the cylinder and the loading gate still open.

"Drop it! You won't make it!"

Billy considered for a second, then let the gun fall.

"Now, get down."

Dismounting, the kid raised his hands. Cope got down and moved to him. In his peripheral vision, he caught sight of the two guards riding up the main trail.

Thinking quickly, he gathered the horses' reins together and pointed to Lauter. "Drag him behind the rocks."

With no choice, Billy complied, lifting his former boss's hands and pulling the limp form behind the specified rocks as Cope followed with the horses.

"Don't you make a sound, Billy." Covering the younger man with his revolver, he crouched and checked Lauter's body for life signs.

Dead—likely from being trampled.

No great loss there.

Riding hard, the guards passed the spot without sighting their quarry, galloping off into the distance in a cloud of dust. Cope breathed a sigh of relief as he watched them go.

"You shoot me, they'll be all over you 'fore you can move. You take me with you, more guards'll stop you." Billy's gaze bored into him like a black storm. There was a smirk on his face. "You're screwed either way, old man."

Son of a bitch!

Cope backhanded him across the face, landing the kid on his butt. He holstered the gun. "I don't have to shoot you, and I don't have to take you with me."

Billy pulled himself up on his elbows. Cope stepped in close and shoved him back to the ground. Stepping over him, he located Billy's right hand, raised his boot and stomped down on it. The satisfying sound of breaking bone crunched from beneath his boot heel. Billy lurched to that side and screamed, but Cope's boot shoved him flat once more and repeated the assault on the left hand.

More screams.

He adjusted his hat on his head. "Now I can leave you right here. Rud Tanner told me all about you, Billy—how you like to play with guns. Well, now you'll never use guns again. Truth be told, in the long run, I likely did you a favor. I know it felt real good to me."

The words were distant to Billy through the anguish of his cries, but in excruciating pain, he made no reaction. Not knowing what to do to ease his agony, he just lay there writhing and whimpering.

Cope stared at this shell of a young man to whom he had just caused unbearable suffering. That was about the right price for the part he played in E.J.'s death.

It wouldn't be long before Billy's cries attracted the attention of the guards, though. Cope mounted and picked up the reins of the packhorse. "*Adios,* Billy."

He returned to the main trail and, urging the horses to a gallop, headed in the opposite direction and kept on going, unconcerned with the anguish he left in his wake.

CIMARRON

10

CLYDE DURESCO RODE HARD, GOING NORTH through the remainder of Texas and across the border between the unorganized territory which contained the Cherokee Outlet and Kansas. He rode even harder crossing the Outlet, trying to stay out of the way of outlaws. *The Outlet's got a reputation for attracting lawbreakers. Vulnerable here. Can't get into Kansas fast enough. Won't do to come all this way only to lose everything to highwaymen.*

Keeping his guns handy and pushing his horse, he covered the fifty-odd miles to the border in a day and a half and found himself coming upon the small, developing community of Liberal, Kansas. *Stock up there and take a rest for a few days.*

During this time, he secured directions to Dodge City and acquired a packhorse to carry a more well-rounded supply cache. He also determined that, because of its size and the type of population it generated, Liberal would serve for nothing more than a stopover.

In contrast to his previous journey, the approximately eighty-mile trip northeast to Dodge took him the better part of five days. Kansas offered more security, however false the premise may have been. There was no hurry covering these miles. It could be done in a much more leisurely fashion. Still, by the time he reached Dodge, he was exhausted. Having little experience on the trail, he did not take to outdoor living, nor did he have the constitution to withstand the long hours and meager food associated with it. First thing he would do is get a filling meal and a comfortable bed upon arrival, before even thinking about what the next move might be.

As he entered Front Street, the main drag of Dodge, he noticed a sign affixed to a wood framed stanchion set in the middle of the thoroughfare. In fact, it was situated in such a way as to be virtually impossible to miss. The message it delivered was short and concise. *The Carrying of Firearms Strictly Prohibited,* it read. Finding this quite incongruous in the place often referred to as a wide-open town, he paused for a second to be sure he read correctly. Satisfied but still confused by it, he moved on to locate a livery at which to board his horses.

Having sequestered the animals and shouldered his saddle bags, he sought out the owner.

"Say, friend, I been on the trail longer than I want to remember. Where's the best place to eat and get a nice soft bed?"

"Yeah, you look plumb wore out. Go on down the street there. Henry's is pretty good. I eats there all the time and ain't keeled over yet. There's a hotel there, too. Ain't sure how the beds is, but I ain't heerd no complaints neither."

Duresco flashed a tired smile. "Much obliged."

He followed the directions, going first to fill his belly.

Savoring each bite of his steak, he made up for lost time and consumed the meal voraciously. As he finished, a heavy-set man in a black coat who wore a badge approached. Duresco made no effort to determine the nature of the medallion, satisfied only that it represented law enforcement.

"Hey, mister, you must be a stranger in Dodge, right?"

Momentarily thrown by the man's boldness, Duresco recovered quickly. Better to cooperate than to piss him off. "That's right. I just got in."

"Figured as much, you carrying a sidearm and all. You'll want to check that at police headquarters or wherever you're staying. And you'll want to do that right quick. You won't want to be caught on the street with it. That'll get you jail time."

Duresco nodded. Appeared to be good advice. "Thanks, officer, I sure don't want that. I'll do as you say."

"Figured you might. Have a good evening now."

Duresco forced a smile and finished his coffee as the officer turned away. Beginning to doubt the efficacy of staying in Dodge, he called to the waiter for the bill. Upon leaving the restaurant, he walked quickly to the hotel, conveniently located next door. As he moved toward the front desk, there was a large sign on the wall above the bald head of the desk clerk stating that handguns could be checked at this location. Getting rid of the gun gave him a strange, comforting feeling, removing the trepidation of having to deal with representatives of the law.

Besides, he still had the backup piece in his vest pocket.

After going through the registration procedure and surrendering his weapon for a claim check, he mounted the steps that led to his room, dropped the saddle bags across a chair and allowed himself to fall into the bed without undressing. He slept until noon the next day.

Awakening abruptly, he needed a second to remember his location before rolling out of bed. He had fallen asleep with his boots on. He pried them off feet swollen during slumber and let them drop to the floor one at a time. He padded to the small mirror attached to the bureau against the wall. His image repelled him. Clothes rumpled, hair in disarray. This would not help him to acquire a table in one of the better gambling halls in Dodge. That required looking the part. He needed not only a bath and a haircut, but a new suit as well.

Doing what he could to temporarily improve his appearance, he squeezed on his boots and exited the room. First stopping at the restaurant for a quick meal, he sought out a bath house and a barber shop, then a haberdasher. By three o'clock, he was a new man as he canvassed the town to examine the multitude of establishments offering games of chance. Passing an entire evening, he found no tables or games available to take over. Frustrated, he approached the bar in the Cattle Queen gambling hall and saloon, the last place he visited.

"What'll it be?" the short, scowling bartender asked as he mopped the bar with a rag that itself needed cleaning.

"Bourbon."

The barkeep reached to the back shelf for a bottle and picked up a glass from the tray under the bar. As he poured the drink, he noticed the dejected expression on Duresco's face.

"Say, what's eating you?"

"I'm looking for a table to take over, but I can't find an open one. I been through the whole town and no luck."

"That's 'cause there's no luck involved. You just don't know the right people."

Duresco sipped the whiskey. The man's words interested him. "Who are these right people?"

"Me, for one. I can get you a table, but it'll cost fifty bucks."

Duresco pondered the proposal. Seemed cheap enough. He could make that and more in a couple of poker hands.

"All right. You put me at a table and you got your fifty."

The bartender winked at him and poured another drink. "Wait here."

Duresco watched as the man left the bar and sought out an expensively dressed overweight individual who stood against the far wall. After a short conversation, he returned with a grin on his face.

"My name's Al. Go see the fat guy over there. Tell him you know me, and you just blew in from St. Louis. He'll set you up."

Duresco smiled as he fished out the money. "Thanks."

Al placed his hand on Duresco's as he placed the money on the bar. "And two bits for the liquor. I ain't in this for my health, you know."

Duresco nodded and produced the cost of the whiskey. He flipped a sloppy salute at Al as he started toward the fat man.

———

RIDING AWAY FROM LAUTERTOWN, COPE, upon determining he was at a safe distance to avoid pursuit, found a suitable campsite in a clearing behind some bushes. While the horses rested, he set up camp. A rest stop, it would last only long enough to replenish himself and his animals. He fed and watered them and, while they remained hobbled and idle, he ate and stretched out for a short nap. But sleep did not come easily. In fact, it did not come at all.

What did come was the weight of that which he had done to Billy Griff. Because of it, he could not shut his mind off. He lay there staring at the sky. In all his years as a peace officer, he'd never done anything as cruel as that. Even more disconcerting, he'd actually enjoyed crushing that kid's hands. Admittedly, he likely *had* lengthened the kid's life by preventing him from the further use of guns, but his intention in doing it had been an act of revenge for his hand in killing E.J.

Worst of all, E.J. would never have approved.

He found himself apologizing to E.J. for allowing his principles to be compromised by his hatred and his desire for reprisal instead of simply bringing the kid to proper justice.

As his final act before continuing his journey, he made a silent promise to her—that he'd keep the balance of this search ethical and lawful.

With that, he moved on.

Stopping in several towns as he rode north, his procedure never changed, replenishment of supplies and coverage of the saloons and businesses to seek information regarding the remaining men he sought. He found no help until he arrived at Liberal, Kansas. There he located the person who had given Duresco directions to Dodge. When Cope showed the man the dog-eared poster, he immediately recognized Duresco as the one he had spoken with a couple of weeks prior.

Cope left Liberal in a hurry and rode hard toward Dodge.

———

ABOUT A WEEK INTO HIS OPERATION as a dealer, Duresco found his earnings much less than expected. Besides having to fork over twenty percent of his take to the house for the use of the facility, he learned that residents of Dodge were quite accustomed to playing a cagey game of poker and quite conservative in their betting habits.

Looking for alternatives, he engaged in conversations with Al, the bartender, learning of a new settlement called Cimarron some twenty miles northwest of Dodge. Having only been in existence for a few months, Al advised that its people were wild and unruly cusses who had money to spend and craved a good time and plenty of excitement. He also passed on that the new marshal there tended to look the other way as long as his pockets were kept full. Duresco took the information to heart.

However, before picking up and moving once again, he decided to give Dodge another chance to pay. This time, his game would be peppered with less than above board tactics.

Thinking himself adept enough to increase his intake, he set his moves in motion.

By midnight, his game had fared much better. Up by five hundred, he decided to go all in and relied on a bottom-dealt hole card. Whether sloppily drawn or the object of sharp observation was unclear to him. Abundantly apparent, however, the hand on his arm that preceded the statement, "That card came from the bottom!"

Duresco's blood ran cold. Son of a bitch! Being a stranger in a town that knew how to deal with cheats, there were very few options available. His cowardice kicked in, save for trying to claim his action as an error. "Sorry, friend. An accident. Must be getting tired. Allow me to divide the pot and run the hand again."

Remarkably tolerant, the players agreed, warning him to keep his hands visible. He divided the pot as suggested and dealt the hand properly. Shit. Lost. The others cashed in, leaving him with an empty table. The fat man came over and summarily dismissed him, advising him to leave Dodge if he knew what was good for him. Wisely following the recommendation, he went immediately to his hotel, packed his things, secured his sidearm and headed west into the darkness without much more than a gain of a few hundred dollars to show for his efforts.

———

COPE ARRIVED IN DODGE AT DUSK a week later and encountered the sign advising against the carrying of guns. Attempting to conduct this by the book, he sought out police headquarters with the intention of identifying himself and his mission and requesting assistance. He was greeted from a desk by the same officer who had advised Duresco to check his pistol.

"Help you, mister?"

Cope nodded. "Name's Worley. I'm looking for two men."

As he spoke, he produced the wanted poster and placed it in front of the detective. The man studied the drawings, then looked up.

"You a bounty hunter?"

"Of sorts. Seen any of them?"

"I'm looking at four men here. Which two?"

Cope indicated the likenesses of Cholla and Duresco without speaking.

"What about the other two?"

"They've been dealt with."

"You kill them?"

"No, just took care of them. Now what about these two? Have you seen them?" This *hombre* was a tad tiresome already.

Still, the other officer persisted. "What's your interest in these men?"

He sighed and pushed his hat back. He reckoned he'd have to give the bugger something before he gave up anything more.

"One of the people killed in that robbery was my wife."

The detective looked Cope in the eye. His expression changed from skepticism to compassion.

"That's different." He pointed to Duresco, "I only saw this one. Ran into him when he first got in. Told him to check his gun. No idea about the other one."

"He still here?"

"I seen him running a game over to the Cattle Queen."

"Where's that?"

The policeman rose. "I'll take you there."

Finally, some cooperation. That was like pulling teeth, but it was better than going door to door. They left the building and headed toward the Cattle Queen. Cope accompanied the detective for several blocks and into the establishment. Upon entering, they split up and scoured the interior for Duresco with no luck.

They met at the bar and Al approached them. "What'll it be, gents?"

Cope again produced the poster. "Seen any of these men in here?"

The bartender looked over the paper. "Don't think so."

The policeman intervened. "This one was running a game in here not too long ago. You saying you didn't see him in here?"

"I don't know. I see lots of folks in here. Maybe."

The officer cleared his throat. "If you don't want to be locked up for obstruction, you better start talking."

Al considered as Cope stared at him. He could see the wheels turning—he wasn't sure about obstruction.

"Yeah, I recollect now." He crossed his arms. "He was dealing here, but he left. Must be about a week back. Said he was heading for Cimarron, I think."

"Where's Cimarron?" Cope asked.

"Settlement about twenty miles west of Dodge," the detective replied. "Only a couple of months old. It's wide open though. Anything goes."

Motivated by this new information, Cope headed for the door, calling out his thanks over his shoulder. As he hit the boardwalk, he pocketed the poster and went to a dead run through the streets back to his horses.

11

DURESCO ARRIVED IN CIMARRON JUST BEFORE dawn. Even in the half-light the outline of the fledgling village was visible on the horizon from several miles out. It was haphazard in construction, as if no thought was given to its design at all. Just a bunch of structures, randomly placed, seemingly for the convenience of the owners.

As he drew nearer, he stopped to observe. Not hard to make out that they were just shacks. Some were just big tents. Most of them likely wouldn't stand up to the Kansas winds. The fact that they were new likely added to their resistance, but he wondered how long it would be before nature won out. No matter. This would *not* be his permanent location. Just a stop off for as long as it took to add some to his stake. But, this time, he had a plan.

He continued into the settlement. Unsurprisingly, nobody was around—too early for them to be up and about.

As he wandered through the jumbled maze—a shack here, a tent there—he looked for a particularly identified building, one that might house the lawman Al had mentioned. That was part of his plan, the insurance part. It took him all of ten minutes to cover the expanse of the minute community.

At the west end of town, he found the tiny wood structure that bore the indiscriminately scrawled sign, *Marshal's Office*. Satisfied that he had accomplished his present mission, he directed his horses toward the only place still showing any activity, a huge tent with an almost illegible marking, *Maizie's Saloon*.

He located a picket line at which several horses were tied and proceeded to secure his animals there. Then, he ventured inside the tent from which piano music and drunken shouts came.

It was a rectangular affair supported by several main poles running down the center and numerous minor shafts shoring up the four-sided canvases that acted as its walls. A slit, acting as a door, in the middle of one of the long walls opened into the huge cavern. Looks like a circus tent like they have back East. Against the far wall, set up on several wooden barrels, a wide plank stretched for about ten feet. Behind that, a wooden stand with two shelves held a line of unlabeled liquor bottles. Beside the shelves, a beer keg with a gravity tap sat on a wooden cradle.

There were improvised tables consisting of smaller planks set up on empty barrels and chairs cobbled together with sticks and rope, strewn around the floor with no particular order. Several survivors of the apparently raucous previous night still sat drinking themselves into oblivion while a few others were already there, either resting their heads on the tables or curled up next to them on the dirt floor. In one corner, an old, hump-backed man in a soiled dress shirt tinkled at an out of tune upright piano and remarkably managed to produce a discernible melody.

Duresco stepped further inside, wondering how these people faired during winter months in this poor excuse for a town. Forget that shit. He'd be headed for warmer places long before the weather changed.

The figure behind the bar drew his attention. A short, overweight woman in her late forties, she appeared much the worse for wear. Dressed in a showy red satin dress with a low-cut bodice that accentuated her ample bosom, she was overly and badly made-up with cheap cosmetics.

This would undoubtedly be Maizie.

"Howdy, stranger, come on in."

Duresco approached the bar. He did this with trepidation, uncertain of that which might follow.

"Have a drink." Her voice was deep and throaty from too much shouting and smoking. Obviously, she imbibed quite a bit during the previous evening, but she seemed well able to hold her liquor. She smiled past a broken tooth. "Only four bits."

He forced a smile. "Yeah. I could use a drink."

She found a glass and a bottle from the shelf behind her and poured one somewhat unsteadily. He dropped the four bits on the plank and downed the liquor.

She looked some better already.

"Maizie's the name." She placed an arm on the bar for support. "What they call you?"

"Clyde."

"Well, welcome to Maizie's, Clyde, where the liquor flows like water and the women are easy and accommodating."

Duresco shuddered. If they're anything like her, he'd pass.

Instead, he simply voiced a thank you.

"You just get in?"

"Yeah. Looking to see if I can set up a table in town. Poker, faro maybe."

"Yeah, you look like the type. Sure, we can arrange that... for a price."

He'd figured that. He smiled charmingly. "I wouldn't have it any other way."

Maizie flashed another leering grin through yellow teeth. "I figured as much. Take that table in the corner. I get ten percent of your take a night."

"Done. What time do you open?"

"Open? Shit, darling, we don't never close!"

———

AFTER A RESTLESS SLEEP IN WHAT Cimarron termed a hotel but which more closely resembled a flop house, Duresco rolled out of his bedroll on the floor and made a successful attempt at standing. A yawn and a long stretch got him started. Stepping out of the tiny building after almost tripping over other sleeping forms, he made his way toward the smell of bacon that wafted through the air. This brought him to an outdoor fire pit over which a huge skillet was frying that bacon. The slovenly fat man tending it informed him that two bits would buy him a platter of the stuff. He flipped the price at the man and grabbed a metal plate, proceeding to take his portion. Having finished it quickly, he headed toward the location he remembered as being the marshal's office. With no idea of the time of day, he rapped on the door and hoped this joker was up.

"Yeah?" a gruff voice on the other side of the door shouted.

Duresco entered hesitantly into a ten-foot square room that contained a small table and chair and nothing more. Behind the table, sat a round-faced man with wide-set, beady eyes and a straight, thin-lipped mouth. His facial hair, while not long enough to be termed a beard, was at least a week old and untrimmed. Covering his graying hair was a narrow-brimmed black hat with a wide leather band. It sat straight on his head and added nothing to his image. His clothes, in need of cleaning, were rumpled. The collarless, striped shirt was bunched under worn suspenders. Duresco eyed him. Not very impressive, but that wasn't the reason he was here.

"What you want?" the man asked in a scratchy, demanding, slurred voice.

"You the marshal?"

"Yeah. Lou Bristow. Who're you?"

"Clyde Duresco. I got a proposition for you."

Duresco allowed Bristow to study him for a second. "What's on your mind, boy?"

"I'm opening a game of chance at Maizie's later today. I'm looking for an insurance policy."

"Like?"

"My games ain't always on the level, see? So, if I get in Dutch, I might need some help to get out of that Dutch, if you catch my meaning."

Now, Bristow showed interest. "Shit like that'll cost you."

"Name a figure."

"Twenty a week'll cover anything you get into." The man wiped his nose with his sleeve. "Including Dutch."

Shit! He was coming up cheap. Couldn't let on to him, though. He might raise the ante. "That's kind of steep, but I guess I got no choice."

"Yeah, no choice. First week now." His hand came out.

Duresco reached into his pocket and handed over a double eagle with feigned reluctance.

Bristow grinned as he pocketed the coin. "I'll be around, if'n you ever get in Dutch."

He left the shack and headed for Maizie's Saloon. Not finding Maizie present, he immediately set up a faro table and waited for interested parties to join him. Not much time elapsed before several transients sat in.

He was on his way.

His prowess with cards served him well over the next week, allowing him to increase his finances by five hundred dollars. Even considering the outlay of Maizie's cut and Bristow's insurance fee, he was doing much better here than in Dodge. While living in this hell hole offered no comfort, he endured it, promising himself that it would not be long before he doubled his holdings. And if he employed some trickery, he could surely shorten his time here. Bristow's "insurance" would protect him from any reprisals.

A new group of buffalo hunters had arrived during the day, increasing Maizie's business. By nightfall, they were liquored up just enough to be looking for a game of chance. Duresco provided that opportunity using a deck of cards he had stacked earlier that day. His wins began at the outset of the game and continued into the evening.

As Bristow entered the saloon for a drink, Duresco raked in a particularly large pot and drew the wrath of one of the hunters who swore he'd seen some sleight of hand perpetrated.

"You're drunk, friend. You're seeing things," Duresco replied to the challenge.

The man grew louder and more accusatory. He came to his feet, producing a skinning knife, and drawing Bristow's attention. Duresco raised his hands in a gesture of innocence as the man started around the table toward him.

Bristow stepped in front of him, sticking a quickly and closely drawn Colt 1860 Army revolver in his ribs. "I want to see you outside."

A look down at the gun settled on his middle convinced him to comply. He placed the blade back in its sheath. Bristow grabbed his arm and turned him toward the opening to the outside of the tent. Now, the pistol was poked into his back.

He went quietly.

As they cleared the slit in the tent, Bristow shoved the hunter into a dark area. He faltered, but maintained his standing position. The marshal raised the pistol and brought it down heavily on the man's skull. With a yelp, he sagged and dropped to his knees. Bristow hit him again.

Falling to his side, the hunter sprawled onto the dirt.

Immediately, Bristow went to a knee and rifled through the man's clothing until he located money. Pocketing it, he rose and went back inside, paying no attention to his victim's condition.

Stepping toward Duresco's table, he winked and moved on to the bar.

Clyde grinned. Problem solved.

The game continued without further interruption.

———

NEAR DUSK, THE DAY AFTER HE left Dodge, Cope came upon Cimarron. With exhausted horses and a grinding hunger, he proceeded warily, trying to arrive inside the village's confines before dark to get a better view of the layout. He hadn't stopped since leaving Dodge—not for food or for sleep—and he was now at the point of weakness from the lack thereof. Still, before he ate or slept, he had to be certain that his quarry was indeed still in town. Once sure of that, he would replenish himself and his stock before making a move.

His horses moved slowly, almost reluctantly, as he entered the settlement. He cast a jaundiced eye about at the shanties and tents and the raucous activities. It was like Deadwood when he'd passed through a few years back. After a thorough examination of the village—including the location of the marshal's office—he headed for the largest den of activity, Maizie's Saloon.

As darkness closed in, he entered the tent and went directly to the bar, finding himself faced by Maizie's leering grin.

"Howdy, there, stranger, welcome to Maizie's. I'm Maizie herself. What's your monicker?"

He'd seen her kind before and knew it was best to give them a wide berth. No good usually came from them, but maybe this one knew the ins and outs of the place. Worth a try.

"Stranger'll do."

"Then Stranger it is. How about a drink?"

"Sour mash."

She reached behind her for the bottle and a glass and poured one out for him.

"Have one yourself."

"Don't mind if I do." She clicked glasses with him and tossed it down like water. Cope sipped his—one step above moonshine, sharp and biting. Taking this in one shot on an empty stomach would likely put him down.

Best to talk first and drink later.

He stretched out his back and glanced around. "Been on the trail near two weeks. Where can I get a steak?"

Maizie leaned on an elbow and gazed at him. "There's folks down the line run a firepit. They cook up a mean one."

"Thanks."

As he took another sip, his gaze settled on the faro table in the corner. Two players sat with their backs to him, but the dealer.... He'd seen that likeness so many times on the wanted poster, there's no need to check it to make sure.

Clyde Duresco.

Too good to be true.

He pointed with the half-full glass. "Is that a closed game over there?"

"Naw," Maizie replied, "it's as wide open as anything else in Cimarron. Go ahead. Sit in."

Confronting Duresco sounded good, but he'd need to have his head in that game. For now, he knew where the bastard was, and, from the looks of him, he'd likely be here awhile. This could wait till he got some food and rest.

He tossed back the rest of the drink. "Believe I'll get that steak first."

Maizie shrugged. "Suit yourself, mister. I'll take a buck for the liquor."

Cope dug out the funds and left them on the bar. He turned for the exit as Maizie scooped up the money. A big, bushy man entered and passed him without stopping. Cope noted the badge but kept going. Something about that *hombre*—call it a hunch, but in that moment, he decided to steer clear of asking for help from the local law. Best handle this alone, at least until Duresco was safely in tow.

12

BY MIDNIGHT, COPE HAD POLISHED OFF a huge steak, seen to the needs of his horses and looked over the dubious accommodations of the local hotel. Deciding that he much preferred the company of his animals over the clientele in that establishment, he collected the horses and brought them to the edge of the town. There he found a pleasant little grove in which he set out his bedroll on a bed of leaves. After hobbling the horses, he lay down and covered himself. Before long, he was fast asleep, a slumber that brought E. J. to him in a dream.

Nothing made sense. Running to catch up to her, but she's not running. Moving away from me but not running, just moving. And the faster I run, the faster she moves, maintaining the same distance from me. He called to her and she looked around. She was smiling but she never stopped moving. Finally, winded, he stopped. Only then, did she stop, that same distance away.

"Why can't I reach you?" he asked her.

"You will, when you're ready." She put her hands on her hips and smiled down at him. "You know what you have to do, Cope, and how you have to do it. It's got to be the right way."

He blinked, and she was gone.

Looking around frantically in the dark, it took him a second to understand that he'd been dreaming. Normally, he did not remember his dreams, even when he first awakened, but this was different. Crystal clear, every detail, every word. And he knew what she meant by "the right way."

What he had done to Billy Griff was unacceptable, at least to E.J. If she was nothing else—and she definitely was many other things—she was just and fair. What he had done wasn't fair, nor was it just. His actions were that of a man slipping into the vengeful type of person he had never been, and she had just called him on it. That was one of the reasons she'd fallen in love with him, his sense of justice and fair play. It had been a match for her own. Now he'd allowed this quest to drag him down to the level of the criminals he'd hunted for so long. He had to keep that in check or he'd be no better than them.

Resolving to heed her warning, he tried in vain to return to sleep.

Finally, after an hour of rolling around to find a comfortable position, he drifted back to sleep and remained in that state, without dreaming, until daylight awakened him. Now rested, hunger became his next concern. After packing up his bedroll, he fed the horses and led them back into town. Picketing them on the line near Maizie's Saloon, he headed back to the fire pit to determine if breakfast was part of their bill of fare.

Biscuits and molasses accompanied the bacon this day. He ordered half a dozen to go with the bacon and sat on the ground near the warmth of the pit to finish them off.

Returning to Maizie's, he took up residence inside to await Duresco's arrival. He found a table and chair and ordered a beer to keep from being accused of taking up space without making a purchase. There he sat for the entire day and some of the early evening.

Shortly after the dinner hour, Duresco arrived to set up shop. Cope watched him arrange the faro box, idly trying to determine if he was stacking the deck. This was purely for diversion's sake. It didn't matter if he cheated or not. Cope's only concern with the man was taking him into custody. Silently, he continued to watch, waiting for the opportunity to execute his plan.

Slowly, players began joining the game until there were four. A few were buffalo hunters, the rest were townspeople—if this rat's nest could even be called a *town*.

An hour and a half passed. Finally, Duresco made the move for which Cope had been waiting. At the end of the current round of play, Clyde excused himself, saying he had to relieve himself. He rose and stepped toward the exit flap.

Cope came to his feet and followed the man outside. Duresco made for a secluded spot toward the end of the tent to conduct his business privately. Cope lifted the revolver from its holster and carried it perpendicular to the ground, hiding it behind his leg.

His gun barrel settled against Duresco's back. "Put it away when you're done. Then don't move a muscle."

Duresco's body stiffened and he pulled in a startled breath. Dutifully, he complied.

Cope took one step to the side as his left hand pulled Duresco's coat away to fetch the revolver from its holster. This he tossed into the bushes. "Turn around slow."

Duresco did it. Cope read the fear in the man's face. Duresco managed to blurt out a sentence, "What do you want?"

"You."

"What do you want me for? I didn't do nothing to you. I don't even know you."

"Name's Worley—and, yeah, you did something to me."

"How could I? I never seen you before."

"Senado Pass. The bank. The woman that was killed while you helped rob that bank. My wife."

The other man's face registered understanding, then fear. Then panic. He turned white and his entire body trembled. "I didn't kill her. Hell, I never even fired a shot. That was Cholla. He done it."

"Yeah, I heard that one before. I'll tell you what I told the others. You were part of it. Makes you as guilty as Cholla."

"W—what you going to do to me?"

"First thought is kill you right here. But E.J. wouldn't like that, so I'll let the law handle it. But, mind you, one crooked move and I'll drop you. Now, head for the marshal's office."

Cope stepped aside to allow Duresco to pass in front of him. Then he stepped in behind and used the gun barrel to direct his charge up the shambles of a street toward Bristow's place. As they passed the saloon tent opening, Maizie's raucous laughter sounded from inside.

During the short walk, Duresco's head was on a swivel, looking for any possibility of escape. While they passed many people, none seemed interested in becoming involved in the affair. They were either involved in their own activities, put off by the gun in Cope's hand, or just plain drunk.

The gambler's gait slowed, prompting Cope to command him to speed up. Not having seen Bristow in the saloon all night, Cope assumed there was a good chance he was in his office. They reached the door.

"In!" He shoved the man's shoulder.

Duresco opened the door and stepped past the threshold. Another shove pushed him off balance and caused him to land on his palms on Bristow's table.

Bristow, seated behind the table, was startled by the interruption. "What the hell—?"

As he spoke, he pushed back from the table and stood

in the same motion, causing the chair to upend behind him. Cope occupied the space of the threshold with his gun leveled on Duresco. Bristow came around the table both confused and angered at the intrusion.

"Got a prisoner for you, Marshal," Cope said.

"Who the hell are you?"

"Cope Worley out of Senado Pass, Texas. This man's wanted for robbery and murder there. I need you to lock him up and arrange to get him back to Senado Pass."

Bristow cocked his head slightly and, after a brief thought, voiced his decision. "Your badge don't mean nothing here."

"I don't carry a badge, Marshal, just a burning desire to see that the men who killed my wife pay for it."

"What—"

Cope took a step inside, crowding the tiny room even more. Reaching inside his shirt, he pulled out the poster and handed it over.

Bristow studied it, then flung the paper to the floor. "This don't mean nothing to me."

"I need him locked up."

"Hey, I'm the marshal here," the older man replied with a growl. "I don't take orders from you."

Cope's patience had plumb worn out. "You son of a bitch! You're nothing but a goddam saloon bouncer with a badge. Now, you lock him up."

"You go to hell, friend. How about I lock you up?"

Cope's gun barrel moved from Duresco to Bristow. "Don't try it."

Unseen by Cope, Duresco lifted his hands from the table and straightened. His right hand made its way into his vest pocket to grip the butt of the Derringer residing there. He cocked the little piece as it came out of the pocket, then spun around to swing the gun into play.

Cope caught it from the corner of his eye. In one motion, he cocked and moved the Colt to Duresco's middle as the Derringer let a round off too early. The slug sang past Cope's head and ended up in the wall behind him.

Duresco wasn't so lucky. Cope's shot found its mark in his belly. Doubling over, the gambler dropped the Derringer and folded to the floor, mortally wounded.

Cope's ears rang under the assault of the gunshots, deafening him completely. Bristow, also temporarily deafened, pulled his sidearm and snapped off a shot that caught the skin of his left forearm. Cope dodged right, cocked, and fired once more. The bullet ground into Bristow's shoulder, spinning him backwards and dropping him into the corner, where he struck his head on the wall. The blow rendered him unconscious.

Shaking his head, he found the Derringer at his feet and kicked it toward the door. He stepped over Duresco's writhing body to Bristow, lifted the gun from the marshal's hand and tossed it over his shoulder. The shoulder wound would be painful, but wasn't life threatening, so he rendered no assistance. He holstered his weapon and returned to Duresco.

Past experience told Cope that the man would not last. Bleeding out from the gut wound, Duresco was even more pale than usual. Even if a doctor was available in this godforsaken hell hole—which he doubted—not much more would be possible than making him comfortable.

"Help me."

Cope ignored the appeal. There was no helping him. He was simply too far gone. Even if he tried, questions would be asked that could hold him back from his search for Cholla. These citizens might not take too kindly to the wounding of their lawman, however crooked he was. No, his only concern had to be locating Duresco's share of the bank money and getting clear of Cimarron before any of this was discovered.

Why did he feel like a damn fugitive all of a sudden?

He rummaged through Duresco's clothes until he located a worn envelope containing the cash in question. Slipping it inside his shirt, he rose and surveyed the damage he'd wrought. None of this had been his fault, but he couldn't help thinking that he'd enjoyed it more'n he should have.

He turned away as Duresco breathed his last.

The tiny gun on the floor attracted his glance. He stooped to pick it up, then hefted it in his hand. That might come in handy sometime. He dropped it in his vest pocket and closed the door behind him. As he left the tiny building, he mulled over in his mind what E.J.'s reaction to this incident might be.

As his hearing began to return, he walked hurriedly to the picket line and untied his horses. No need to attract undue attention. Mounting quickly, he checked the stars for direction and then headed west, away from Cimarron.

A short distance out, he pulled up and glanced over his shoulder. If anybody had asked, he'd have said he was checking for any trailers. In reality, though, he was still considering the legitimacy of that which he had just done... and the results still disturbed him.

He rode on.

GOD'S
ACRES

13

AFTER SPLITTING THE MONEY WITH HIS cohorts, Lorenzo Cholla headed northwest through Texas, New Mexico Territory and into Colorado. He had no particular destination in mind. His plan was to maintain a low profile and keep moving. He wanted to put enough distance between himself and Senado Pass to be clear of any connection with the bank incident. He had no idea that he had been identified and was now the subject of a private manhunt.

He had new country to see and new adventures in which to engage, and the legality or lack of same made no difference to him. The bank money acted as his savings, of sorts, something to fall back on, but, by no means, the last he would acquire. On the contrary, it was just the beginning. The right situation would allow him to generate funds on a continuing basis. He would take it from there.

Just over the border between Texas and New Mexico, he learned, in the first New Mexican town he came upon, that his present route would take him through untamed areas inhabited by rogue bands of Comanche. These had yet to be rounded up by the Army, and so, roamed relatively freely, threatening travelers. The knowledge prompted him to look into adding to the meager fire power that his .30 caliber Colt handgun currently afforded him. His search turned up a .52 caliber Spencer carbine which was touted as being accurate at over five hundred yards. This precision and the seven-shot capacity would suffice to protect him. The fortunate—if overpriced—acquisition allowed him to proceed with reasonable safety.

Continuing to travel in a northwest direction, he made his way through the heart of the territory without incident. Twenty days on the trail put him near the Colorado border and tired him to the point of exhaustion. He needed to rest before continuing and spent three days in a small border town.

During his visit, he learned of the benefits available in Denver. Businesses were thriving there and employment was abundantly available. According to his sources—one of whom was the local law enforcement officer—the city was rich and the opportunities were plentiful.

He headed for Denver.

———

FOUR DAYS INTO HIS NORTHBOUND TRIP into Colorado, Cholla descended the San Juan Mountains into the San Luis Valley, a high-altitude, desert-like basin. The arid conditions gave him pause to be thankful for the barrel of water lashed to his pack animal. As he proceeded, he became aware of dust rising in the distance. Since no wind existed at present in the area, he ruled out dust devils which he had witnessed in Texas. Must be something else. Glancing around, he found no protection offered by the level ground covered only by a low, woody brush that grew close to the surface. Still, he kept going. Maybe that cloud would be of little consequence.

Moving another mile forward, the disturbance showed no sign of abating. The unmistakable sound of gunfire reached his ears. He pulled at the reins, stopping his horses, and strained his eyesight to get a clearer picture of the occurrence. All he could make out at this point was that the dust was moving toward him. Seems to be coming on pretty fast. More shots split the quiet. That was rifle fire.

As his concern increased, the scene resolved into a Conestoga wagon being drawn by a six-horse team and driven furiously by a black coated individual. On its heels, at least four and possibly more Comanche galloped hard to overrun their quarry. Three of them had rifles—single shot pieces. The others carried lances, bows, and arrows.

They were coming on too fast. He dismounted and secured the reins of both horses to rabbitbrush. Immediately, he pulled the Spencer from its saddle sheath and went to a knee to project the smallest target possible. First time using this piece in battle. Up to now, it had been good for hunting. He hoped the accuracy held under these circumstances.

Shouldering the gun and focusing on the front site, he swept it left to engage the lead rider, cocked it and let this first round fly. With a great boom and the kick of a mule, the big rifle fired a huge cloud of smoke and belched out a round that burrowed into the rider's chest with enough force to unseat the man from his mount and send him smashing to the ground.

As the other warriors became aware of this act, Cholla levered the weapon and leaned into another shot. A second rider was knocked soundly from his horse.

By this time, the wagon rushed past him, spewing dirt and dust in its wake. This made aiming another shot almost impossible. Still, he levered and prepared to fire. A lance imbedded itself in the ground only inches from his knee. Behind it, a warrior rode at full gallop toward him, intending to take him down. He swung the muzzle in that direction and pulled the trigger at the dusty outline of the figure. Between the existing dust and the black powder smoke generated by the shot, he could not determine if he hit the mark. Then the horse loped past him without its rider. He must have gotten him.

Levering another round to the ready, he strained to see through the now dissipating dust and was rewarded with the sight of the remaining Comanche turning tail and collectively leaving the scene. He lowered the rifle to his hip and got to his feet, his heart slamming with the adrenaline rush. The dust cleared sufficiently to show that the attackers continued to flee, heading toward the mountains. Was this the end of it, or just a lull? He had to get out of this open area.

Grabbing the reins of his mount, he swung into the saddle and reached to loosen the pack animal. Seating the rifle in its scabbard, he led the packhorse toward the wagon which was pulling up. As the wagon came to a stop, he sided it and drew rein, laying eyes on the driver up close for the first time.

The man on the driver's seat was tall. This could be seen even seated. Lanky, one might even term him skinny, with a gaunt, sunken, clean shaven face that had great crags and protruding bones. In a black, flat-crowned hat and black frock coat, his manner of dress gave the impression he could be an undertaker.

"You are a godsend, sir," he said in a deep croaking voice. "May the Lord bless you, my son, for your timely intervention."

Cholla smiled and he patted the butt of the rifle. "I'm not sure the Lord had anything to do with it, unless His name is Spencer."

"His name is Jesus Christ, sir, and I'm sure He sent you." The man leaned backward to breathe a sigh of relief. "My name is Rupert Armitage. May I know who has delivered me from evil?"

Taken unaware, Cholla stumbled for a second.

"Oh, eh... Lawrence... Lawrence Chilton. Those savages

just might try to get us again. We should get clear of this open space as quick as possible."

"I do believe you're right, Mr. Chilton."

"Safety in numbers. Head for the rocks over there."

Sighting the rock outcropping to the right at which Cholla pointed, Armitage whipped up the team and directed them toward it hurriedly. Cholla fell in behind, constantly checking over his shoulder for signs of the raiding party. Armitage pulled the team up close to the rocks.

Cholla came alongside once more. "Try to get the wagon in front of that little carve-out there," he said. "We can use the wagon for cover and wait it out to be sure it's safe before moving on."

"Excellent," Armitage replied.

Maneuvering the wagon expertly into position, he stopped the team as Cholla dismounted and began releasing the horses from harness. "We'll bring the horses inside to protect them."

Armitage climbed down from the seat and assisted him. Within minutes, all the animals had been herded into the small depression beside the wagon. Cholla pulled the Spencer free and placed himself at a point in the rocks from which he could safely view the area in which the skirmish had taken place. With the dust now cleared, the bodies of the three Comanche he shot were visible. He concentrated his sight on that section.

"Do you think they'll come back?" Armitage asked, somewhat warily.

"They'll come to collect their dead, I'm sure. We'll see what they do after that."

They waited and watched for approximately ten minutes, during which Cholla fed more cartridges into the spring-loaded tube in the butt of the Spencer. When no more would fit, he closed the hatch and levered a round into the chamber.

"I'm sorry you had to do that, Mr. Chilton," Armitage said, almost as a spoken private thought.

"Do what?"

"Kill those Comanches. I feel it's my fault. It weighs heavily on my mind."

"I don't remember having much choice in the matter. How is it your fault?"

"The mere fact that I was here, on their land."

"It's not their land anymore, Mr. Armitage. You've got just as much right to be here as they have."

"Still, it is a sin against God's law to take another's life."

"Some might argue that point. First I saw of you, I pegged you for an undertaker. But you're not, are you?"

"Why, no. I'm a duly ordained Baptist minister. I was traveling through this land on my way to establish a church in the Utah Territory. A place called God's Acres."

"Interesting. Well, that would explain it."

Cholla's words did not reveal his thought process. Although not fully developed, the glimmer of an idea concerning Armitage started taking shape.

His attention was again drawn to the combat site as, in the distance, the band of warriors approached.

"Mr. Armitage," he asked, "do you own a gun?"

"Why, yes, an old rifle I use for hunting. It's in the wagon. Why do you ask?"

"You might want to dig it out. We're getting company."

Armitage climbed to the wagon seat and stepped inside. In a few seconds, he emerged carrying an old percussion piece, a powder horn and a bag holding shot. Climbing down, he took up a spot close to the area Cholla occupied. As distasteful as this act seemed to him, he apparently chose to fight, if necessary, alongside the man who had saved him and now sought to protect them. He knelt to pray silently as he loaded the weapon.

Trying to give the impression that he'd done this type of thing before, Cholla kept watch as the Comanche continued to approach slowly, leading unoccupied horses. Upon reaching the place of the conflict, they congregated around the bodies of their fallen comrades. Several dismounted and lifted the dead onto horses. These men remounted, and the group remained in place, appearing to train their gazes on the wagon in the distance. Clearly, they could see that the horses had been detached and they seemed to understand the danger waiting behind the wagon. Discussion ensued for several minutes.

Cholla observed as the warriors made no secret of their desire to resume the attack. Looks like they're debating this. He waited to see what the determination would be. If they did attack, they had enough numbers to outlast a two-man defense. They'll know they were in a fight, no matter what the outcome.

Tense moments later, the Comanche made their decision. Slowly, they turned away from the location of the wagon and began moving as a group toward the horizon. Their manner indicated they would not return.

Both men breathed a sigh of relief at the sight.

Cholla unseated himself from his perch and joined Armitage. "Let's get out of here fast before they change their minds."

Quickly assembling and harnessing the horses to the wagon, they set out to the west, searching for a route through the mountains. Without advising Armitage, Cholla decided to stay with his new companion, discarding his desire to reach Denver, as a new plan developed in his mind. Armitage did not question Cholla's selection.

———

A FEW DAYS INTO THE JOURNEY west across the valley, they observed a change in the lay of the land. Desert barrenness gradually transitioned into conditions more suitable for habitation and agriculture.

As they crested a rise about a mile into that area, they came upon a small settlement that also appeared to be in a state of flux. They noted wagons in a cluster at the beginning of the installation seemingly circled into a camping arrangement. Further ahead in the distance were the skeletons of buildings in various stages of development, and the sound of hammering and sawing came faintly from those locations.

Drawing rein at the top of the rise, they scrutinized the scene.

"Looks like they're building a settlement here," Armitage said. "Perhaps we can rest here. Shall we investigate?"

"Why not?" Cholla replied.

The way Armitage interacted with mixed company interested Cholla, as part of building the mental file on the clergyman for use at a later time.

They moved down the slight hill toward the group of wagons. The aroma of meat cooking reached their nostrils. With no opening between the parked wagons large enough to drive through, Armitage stopped outside the circle and climbed down from the seat. Cholla dismounted and secured his reins to the tailgate. Together they entered the camp.

In the center of the ring of wagons, a large fire had been built over which several deer carcasses were being roasted. Around the fire, several men and women tended the cooking. Some noticed the strangers approaching and called the attention of a thin man with a ragged white beard and mustache. He was inordinately tall with a long neck and a bony, craggy face that caused him to somewhat resemble Armitage. Dressed in worn, nondescript clothing and a battered hat, he responded to the alert by turning to the visitors.

"Good day, friends," he said in a scratchy baritone voice that betrayed his age. "Welcome."

"Hello," Armitage replied, approaching the man and extending his hand. "We were passing and saw your settlement."

"Please come in. We're building a new home here and all are welcome to join us. My name is Elijah Talbot. I guided these people here. Welcome to our community."

Armitage shook hands with Talbot as he spoke. "A new community. I'm very heartened by this news. I'm Rupert Armitage, a Baptist minister, on my way to establish a church in a place that I think may be very similar to what you have here. This is my traveling companion, Mr. Chilton."

Cholla shook hands with Talbot and nodded a silent greeting.

"I'm very happy to meet you both," Talbot said through a grin. "Please join us. Eat with us. Stay as long as you like."

"You're most kind, Mr. Talbot," Armitage replied. "Indeed, we are in need of some rest and nourishment before we continue."

"Then you shall have that, sirs."

Talbot made introductions and the people around the fire welcomed them. When the venison was ready, they were included in the meal. One inhabitant went to summon those who worked on the outlying structures and those people came back and joined in the community meal.

During conversations, some small excitement ensued when the people learned of Armitage's calling. A minister was one of the assets missing from the community. Talbot made an offer for the preacher to stay on and tend to their spiritual needs.

"I can see the need you have for someone of faith," Armitage told the gathered community. "And I am very gratified that you think me qualified to serve. However, I must honor my commitment to go on to God's Acres, so I must decline. Is there anything I can do for you during the time I'm here?"

Several people asked him to bless the homes they were building. With those requests spoken, more members of the community echoed the desire.

"I would be happy to invoke the Lord's blessing on every structure and on every person here. That is the least I can do to repay the warm welcome you have extended us. Shall we begin in the morning?"

His offer met with a rousing affirmative response.

After a restful night's sleep near the fire, morning found Armitage up early and making ready to travel to the construction sites to fulfill his promise. Cholla rolled out a little later but hurriedly prepared to accompany Armitage. Talbot joined them, and they proceeded to each individual build at which Armitage audibly prayed for blessings on the people and the structures as well as the success of the efforts of the community. Cholla paid extremely close attention to the mannerisms, the words and the intonation used by Armitage, filing these carefully into his memory. The process consumed most of the morning at which point they returned to the main camp. After consuming a meal, Cholla and Armitage prepared to leave.

Before they left, Talbot made one more attempt to persuade Armitage to stay on.

"No, I'm sorry," Armitage replied from the seat of the wagon. "I must fulfill my commitment. I thank you for your hospitality and wish you well in the future."

"And you, Mr. Chilton? You're equally welcome to stay," Talbot said.

Cholla, whose plan involving Armitage continued to take shape, chose his words carefully as he mounted and prepared to ride. "I feel sort of connected to Mr. Armitage. He's become part of my life. I'll see this through with him."

14

TRAVELING BLINDLY, COPE CONTINUED WEST. He kept in the back of his mind the direction Chunky Bond had indicated as being Cholla's last known choice, northwest. Reasoning that a westerly course might hold out some hope for intersecting with Cholla, he kept going. With stops in towns along his path yielding no further information, he found himself entering Colorado. Some of this country was familiar to him, causing a plan to form in his mind. He changed to a southwesterly direction to re-enter New Mexico.

Not five miles in, he located the spot he sought, a tiny village called Spilsbury. He was acquainted with the local law officer there and he hoped he would be able to gain some advantage from this visit. Spilsbury was on a straight northwest line from Senado Pass. Cholla might have passed through. A long shot at best, but anything seemed better than the nothing he had now.

His entrance into Spilsbury was slow. Exhausted and in need of nourishment, as soon as he hit this one-street village, both requirements came to the forefront. Had he not arrived at the constable's quarters first, he would have stopped at the first place in which he could procure a hot meal. But first things first. He drew rein in front of the small clapboard building and came heavily out of the saddle. No hitch rail. He used a porch post to secure both horses and sauntered to the door.

Enoch Quince looked up from his paperwork as the door opened and a ragged figure stepped in.

"Howdy, Enoch."

There was some degree of recognition in Quince's face, but Cope's beard and dusty clothes and hat likely increased the difficulty.

"Howdy yourself," he said automatically in an age-tinted voice, but then continued somewhat puzzled. "Wait. Do I know you?"

Cope closed the door and removed his hat. "It's me, Enoch, Cope Worley."

These words caused instant identification. Quince came out of his seat abruptly. "Why, Cope. Holy smoke, I ain't seed you in a month of Sundays."

"Yeah, it's been a while." Cope regarded this man, who had not changed a bit, in the few years since their last encounter. He was a little older and bent over a bit more, but the long, mustached face and the close-set, wide eyes that added a constant look of amazement remained the same. He had a tad less hair and it was grayer, but basically, Enoch was unchanged.

"Come on in," Quince said. "Set a spell. Say, you look plumb tuckered out, like you been riding for months. What's going on?"

Cope did not answer immediately, but instead, moved slowly to an unoccupied chair near Quince's desk. "Not a social call, Enoch. I need some help. I'm tracking a man."

Quince sat down. "Always willing to help a fellow lawman, Cope. You know that. What can I do?"

Quince's reference to his being a lawman backed him up. He needed to know that Cope was just a civilian now.

"Reckon you haven't heard. I don't have the badge anymore. I'm doing this on my own. The man I'm hunting killed my wife."

Quince was noticeably moved by this information. "Your wife? Aw, Cope, I'm sure sorry to hear that. How'd it happen?"

Cope took a deep breath and proceeded to relate the story of E.J.'s demise. He was visibly shaken by the time the tale was complete. Quince reacted with sympathy and resolve.

"Nobody should ought to have to go through that, Cope. What can I do to help?"

Cope pulled forth the poster, now dog-eared, and handed it to Quince. The images of Lode, Duresco and Billy Griff had been crossed out leaving only Cholla's picture untouched.

"Upper left. That's the man that killed E.J. Any chance you seen him of late?"

Quince studied the image carefully. He appeared to be digging into his memory for assistance. Moments passed silently. Then his face registered recollection. "Son of a bitch! He was here—here in Spilsbury! Not two weeks ago. He rode in asking after where he could locate business opportunities. Folks told him to go to Denver, me included. Cope, I swear, if I'd have knowed who he was, he'd already be in custody or dead."

Heartened by this news, but sensing Quince's frustration, Cope told him, "I'm sure of that, Enoch, but you couldn't know. Did he head for Denver?"

"Said he was. I reckon as much."

"Thanks."

Cope reached and retrieved the paper. Replacing it in his pocket, he withdrew the money he had taken from Duresco's body and placed it on the desk.

"This is part of what was taken from the bank. Got it from the last *hombre* I nailed. I need you to wire it back to Senado Pass. Send it care of Sheriff Rud Tanner. Tell him it's from me. He'll see to it."

"Consider it done, my friend."

Cope rose and started toward the door.

"You heading for Denver?"

"I am. Thanks for your help."

"Wisht I could side you."

"Thanks, Enoch, but you don't want to be anywhere near me when I get Cholla in my sights."

Quince seemed to know what was behind Cope's words. He offered a caution. "You be careful. You ain't got the badge to back you up no more."

Cope stopped for a second to reflect on the constable's admonition. "You're the second man to give that warning, Rud Tanner being the first. Same as I told him. It don't matter. Nothing matters but getting Cholla."

He stepped through the doorway, leaving Quince as wide -eyed as when he had entered. The thought occurred to Cope to head out now, but he would need every ounce of energy for the coming trip. True of his horses as well. A quick meal and a night's rest for all three were in order. He found a stable that provided for the animals and used the hay in an unoccupied stall to rest. Too tired to seek out a hot meal, he consumed some jerky. After a restless night, he set out at dawn, heading directly north.

His path was not as straightforward as Cholla's had been. Once across the New Mexico border and into Colorado, he found it necessary to scale mountainous regions that made his attempt to stay true north difficult. Pushing his animals almost to their limits, he emerged from these hilly areas into the western side of the San Luis Valley. As he came out of the foothills, the establishing community which Cholla and Armitage had visited loomed before him. Although a deviation would take him off his chosen course, he would stop and question the inhabitants. Hurriedly, he changed direction and made for the settlement, heading into a fairly strong breeze that caused him to tug at his hat brim to insure it stayed properly seated.

Elijah Talbot swung an axe at the portion of a log that stood on a knee-high tree stump, splitting it clean in half. He stood outside the circle of wagons at the east end of the new community. As the split wood fell to the ground, Talbot prepared to set another piece on the chopping base, but movement coming from the south caught his attention. While the image was too far to discern, he stopped his task to study it closer. Within moments he made out a rider leading a packhorse. Curious, he sank the axe into the stump to await the arrival of this stranger.

Cope spotted the tall man with the axe from quite a distance away. Looks to be peaceful enough. He continued at his previous pace as he watched the man assume a stance indicating only curiosity but no apprehension. Planning no prolonged visit, Cope drew rein within several feet of where Talbot stood, but remained mounted.

"I bid you good day, friend," Talbot said pleasantly with the wisp of a smile through his beard. "Won't you step down and rest a spell?"

"Thanks, but I'm in kind of a hurry."

Cope immediately pulled the ragged poster from his shirt and leaned over to hand it to Talbot. The wind made it difficult to keep it open.

"I'm looking for the fellow shown there called Cholla. Seen him?"

Talbot took the paper and unfolded it, studying the images. "Why these others be crossed out?"

"Not looking for them anymore, just Cholla. Seen him?" Tired, he had no intention of wasting time on curious questions. He wanted answers.

Talbot seemed to pick up on Cope's sense of immediacy

and examined the picture more carefully. His scrutiny yielded results. "I know this man, but not by this name."

"What name did he use?"

"Called himself Chilton. Yeah, Lawrence Chilton, that's the name." Talbot hesitated a second before he continued. "He was traveling with a minister name of... Ar—Armstrong? Armitage? That's it, Armitage. They stopped here a few days. The minister blessed our little community here and they moved on."

"Which way?" Cope asked with renewed interest.

"West, through the mountains there. Reverend Armitage said he was going to a place in Utah to settle. Place called God's Acres. I remember that real good 'cause it's such an odd name for a town."

Now, he was chomping at the bit. His first solid lead on Cholla and he would not let it go. "How were they traveling? Horse? Wagon?"

"The minister had a covered wagon. Chilton—Cholla—he was riding a big white horse."

"How long past?"

"A week, maybe two. No more'n two."

Talbot held the poster out. At the instant Cope grabbed for it, Talbot let loose, and the wind quickened and assumed control of the paper. It swished it away, out of the grasps of both men.

"Sorry," Talbot said.

"No matter."

"Say, what do you want with—" As Talbot spoke, Cope pulled his horse's reins and set out at a near gallop toward the mountainous region to the west. "—this fellow Chilton—Cholla—anyhow...?"

Gone before the question was finished, Cope never answered.

———

WENDING THEIR WAY THROUGH THE MOUNTAIN passes, Cholla and Armitage continued to push west. Armitage referred several times to a map and list of directions that accompanied the letter from God's Acres accepting his candidacy to lead the spiritual health of that settlement. Using these, they stayed on the correct course when route questions arose. Cholla made certain he always knew the location of these documents. He would need them later in the journey. He also continued to closely observe Armitage's actions and body language as well as his speech patterns under different circumstances, mentally filing them for future reference.

As they emerged from the mountains into the foothills of southwestern Colorado near the Dolores River, they came upon a small settlement consisting of some eighty inhabitants and several makeshift clapboard buildings. Being close to a bend of the river, it was called Big Bend. After the rough terrain they had just endured, Cholla and Armitage individually found no need to engage in discussion regarding whether a stop should be made. They simply and silently made straight for the town.

Their stay in the tiny village was short. They replenished their stores from the meager supplies the businesses had available and rested their animals and themselves overnight. During this brief respite, Cholla continued to observe Armitage's interactions with the residents and amassed more to memorize for future use. Armitage verified their path to Utah and expressed appreciation for the hospitality provided. They were assured that they could reach the vicinity of God's Acres within a two-week period. The next morning found them up early and back on the trail in short order.

———

COPE'S PUSH THROUGH THE MOUNTAINS WAS relentless and exhausting, both for himself and his animals. Had he not attached the gravity to this mission that it now bore, he would have been gentler on himself and the horses, but he was too close now to take a softer line. Early on, in the foothills, he had picked up recent wagon tracks which he attributed to the minister's conveyance. Along with these, he found hoof prints in the softer ground of an accompanying rider that he took to be Cholla. While none of this was a certainty, if he pressed forward with additional speed, he might stand a chance of catching up to them.

He had to try to avenge E.J.

At least, he told himself that initially. But the more he studied on it, the more apparent it became that his own satisfaction was at the core, so he had the chance to make Cholla pay. This became the driving force behind his push through some of the roughest country he had ever traveled.

From time to time, he found patches of softer ground on which the appearance of wheel tracks and hoof prints bolstered his belief in this being the correct route. At several junctures, brief glimpses of this familiar trail answered the question of which way to proceed.

His eventual exit from the huge rocks put him on the path to Big Bend. The tracks confirmed that those he sought had headed for that same location. This added impetus to his drive.

His entry into the settlement was low key and unassuming. Uncertainty as to the presence or absence of Cholla in this place caused him to remain in the shadows until the answer could be obtained. He used care in observing the inhabitants of each building before entering and then attempted to blend with these people when he did. Using these cautions, he vetted each location before questioning anyone regarding Cholla and the minister.

When he satisfied himself that his overtures would not

forewarn his potential target, it became necessary, because of the loss of the poster, to speak in generalities. His question now became, "Have you seen a minister driving a covered wagon traveling with a man on a white horse?"

Several residents replied in the affirmative, informing him that two such men had passed through Big Bend several days earlier heading west to Utah. These answers caused him to scramble to get back on the trail. Apparently, he was gaining on them and he fully intended to maintain or better that advantage. Maybe, at this pace, he would be able to overtake them before they made it to Utah.

———

THE SIGN ON THE SIDE OF the trail, rudimentary as it was, indicated with an arrow the direction of Utah. Aware they were now within miles of the goal, Armitage smiled and uttered a prayer of thanks to his God for delivering him safely this far. Cholla also noticed the single worded marker. Time to execute the next step in the plan. Now, to develop the specifics that would accomplish this purpose.

To this end, he concocted a situation into which Armitage could be easily drawn. Meat was in short supply, necessitating a hunt to replenish the stores.

Cholla, in front of the wagon team, caught sight of something in the distance and raised his hand to signal a halt to Armitage. The minister drew rein and stopped the wagon. Cholla continued looking into the expanse before them.

"I see something."

"What is it?"

Cholla turned his horse and returned to the side of the wagon. He pointed to the forestry to the side of the trail. "Looked like a deer up in the woods there."

"We could use the meat," Armitage replied.

"We should both make a try for him, from different sides."

"I'll get my rifle." Armitage reached into the wagon and retrieved the old gun.

"You go in from here," Cholla said, "I'll ride up the trail and come in behind him. Maybe we can close in on him and flush him out."

Armitage began climbing down from the seat, "All right."

Cholla turned his horse and hurried up the trail as Armitage trotted into the trees on a perpendicular path from the wagon. Quickly, Armitage disappeared into the woods.

When he was convinced that Armitage had engaged in the hunt, Cholla again turned his horse and rode back to the wagon. Dismounting, he secured his reins to the wheel, grabbed his rifle and followed Armitage.

Once in the wooded area, Cholla moved in a straight line until he caught sight of Armitage. Looks like he's fully involved in the hunt, not paying any attention to anything around him. Cholla moved in on Armitage with as much stealth as he could muster.

An experienced hunter, Armitage quickly spotted the deer and dropped to a knee for a more stable shooting position. As he raised the rifle to his shoulder, Cholla loomed suddenly behind him. A quick, well-placed swipe with the stock of the weapon landed a telling blow behind Armitage's right ear, reeling him to the ground senseless.

Startled by the sound, the deer bolted. Not wishing to lose much needed food, Cholla shouldered the gun and sighted on the running animal. One shot brought it down. Cholla then returned his attention to Armitage who was now regaining consciousness. Another swing of the butt hit the minister alongside his head, again rendering him out cold. Blood streamed profusely from both wounds as Cholla worked feverishly to pull the clothes from Armitage's body. Again, Armitage stirred as the last article of clothing was tugged free. Cholla bunched the garments together on the ground a safe distance away from the incident and then placed the rifle across the bundle to keep the garments in place. As he turned, Armitage attempted to raise his body on his elbows. Still mostly out of it, he managed to start regaining his feet as Cholla drew his revolver, which seemed quicker than reaching again for the rifle. He raised and cocked the piece. At this close distance, aiming was unnecessary.

Reeling and unsteady, but still lucid, Armitage registered recognition of his assailant and uttered one word as Cholla fired from the hip.

"Why—?"

The bullet caught him in the lower torso. Its force doubled him over and deposited him on his back, spread-eagled. Cholla turned quickly and scooped up the clothing. He returned to the wagon to drop them off and headed back to collect the deer carcass and the rifle. Perfect. It accomplished the initial mission and the deer became an unexpected but welcome supplement.

Not bad for a plan conceived on-the-fly!

15

HOURS AFTER CHOLLA'S DEPARTURE FROM THE
scene of his latest transgression, Armitage returned
to a slight semblance of his senses. Terrible pain
became an immediate and unwelcome companion, combined
with weakness the likes of which he had never known. It was
clear he was dying. While not frightened at this prospect, his
instinct for survival kicked in as more of his senses returned.
He had the work, to help the souls of God's Acres, and the fear
that Lawrence Chilton, not who he professed to be, might hurt
others if not stopped. These two facts drove him to struggle to
last just a little longer.

As lucidity slowly returned, he attempted to assess his
situation. His head, although still functioning, throbbed with
pain. The gnawing anguish in his torso told him this was the
telling wound, the one that would kill him. The life slowly
ebbed from him as he lost irreplaceable blood. Amazingly, his
mind still worked.

Flat on his back in the middle of a forest did not help his
situation. He needed to get back to the trail where his chances
of being discovered would be infinitely better. Time and

strength were limited and decreasing by the minute. He had to make that move now.

Looking around to get his bearings and finding that everything took on a different appearance, he took a moment to focus. The first item he spotted was the rifle, within what seemed to be a few feet away. That weapon was vital to his move. Although it only carried one round, it might be needed to ward off scavengers.

With the greatest effort and the highest pain level he had ever endured, he forced a leg to bend and a foot to dig into earth as a wedge. Continuing this struggle and allowing cries of suffering to issue forth from his throat, he pushed harder than he had ever done before to roll his body onto his stomach.

Once he accomplished that, he took a moment to deal with the increased pain and dizziness incurred by the act. Getting a handle on this renewed level of pain, he waited until his head cleared enough for navigation. He took it in steps, this monumental effort that might ultimately help him survive.

Pulling himself with his elbows and arms and assisting that endeavor with his one operable leg, the other inexplicably useless, he accomplished something resembling a low crawl. This moved him to the rifle. Gripping the weapon, he forced his body to continue hauling itself in the direction of the road. Unable to see clearly because of the irregular terrain, he hoped this was the right direction. He kept moving until he reached the edge of the woods and then looked up to see the trail. Exhausted, he allowed himself to stop to catch his breath and try to renew his strength and resolve. During these few moments, he uttered a quick prayer requesting the wherewithal to continue.

Uncertain if due to the answer to his prayer or the resilience of his own body, he became able, within a few minutes, to push on. If anything could be considered excruciating torture, this was it. Nothing in his life had equaled or prepared him for this test. But his determination held as, hand over hand with the help of the foot, he moved forward. Screams pointed up the terrible pain. Frequent stops were necessary to replenish his fading strength and will, but, finally, he made it. At last, he reached the middle of the trail. As he looked around for nonexistent assistance, complete exhaustion took over, placing him in the black void of nothingness.

———

COPE'S RELENTLESS PACE CONTINUED. DRIVEN BY the conviction he was gaining on Cholla, based on information gathered from settlements and camps along the route, he pressed harder. No longer taking time to rest himself in these places, he only allowed the duration required to replenish supplies and care for his animals. Then, back on the trail, pushing the horses to their limit and constantly following wagon tracks and new leads.

By now, beyond ragged in appearance, his clothes were soiled and torn, and his body was crusted with dirt and dust that had stuck to sweat. Leaving no time to care for himself, he mimicked the trail bums he had encountered at Cimarron. But he no longer cared about that.

The only thing in his mind was Cholla, tracking down Cholla, killing Cholla. Sleeping only when he needed to, this purpose drove him day and night. When he did sleep, he dreamt of E.J. and tried to ignore her spirit's admonishments. To forget this quest. To make a new life for himself. Stop now before he became no better than the man he was hunting. She was right on all points, but his determination and hatred constantly won out and bade him to press on. He was too close to give up now.

Convincing himself his function resembled that of a lawman, he viewed this as a public service. Never mind the fact that it would satisfy his thirst for revenge, this eliminated a law breaker who would definitely offend again.

Midday approached. Cope had already been on the trail for five hours. Got to stop to eat. The wagon tracks seemed as fresh as they had been for days. He failed to see himself gaining on his objective and decided that time permitted only a piece of jerky taken in the saddle. Reaching behind to procure the food from his saddle bag, his eye caught sight of something in the road ahead. Too far to be a clear image, but there was definitely something there, something that shouldn't be there. Deferring sustenance, he kicked his heels into the horse's flanks to gain more speed, dragging the packhorse reluctantly along.

Not bothering to estimate the distance to the object, Cope rode harder and strained his vision to identify it. The outline of a body was positioned face-down in the middle of the road. Concern and curiosity forced him to urge more speed from the tired horses.

As he drew nearer, features of the figure became clearer. If it was Cholla, it was done.

God, how he hoped so.

The sight of gray hair and a slender build argued against this, though.

He rode at a lope to within several feet of the form and then pulled up sharply and dropped from the saddle.

As he stepped forward cautiously, no movement was visible. Dead, maybe. Most curious about this man, the fact that he was clad only in a union suit and frayed socks. What happened to this *hombre* and where were his clothes?

Going to one knee by the body, Cope checked the jugular for a pulse, noting the two individual head wounds. Blood was comingling in the gray hair.

Faint pulse. Not dead, but damn close.

Glancing around, he took in the splotches of blood on

the dirt road. His eyes followed them back toward the woods. Whatever happened likely took place in there and he hauled himself to here.

Cope stood up and went to his horse to retrieve the canteen. Returning, he gently rolled the man onto his back. The sight of the belly wound stopped him cold.

Gut shot.

Painful way to die. Took some grit to pull himself out here after a wound like that.

Reaching down, Cope lifted the man's head and propped it against his own leg and then dribbled some water across the parched lips. Dumping some water on his hand, he patted the forehead to revive the man. After a few seconds, it worked.

The eyes fluttered, opening and closing several times before sense began a slow and still distant return. He looked around absently as Cope leaned in to allow more water to drop onto his lips. Instinctively, they opened slightly and took in some of the fluid. Cope backed the canteen off immediately.

"Not too much." He'd done this before.

The man swooned, but managed to swallow the water. Sparingly, Cope offered more. After several like episodes, the man became more aware although so weak he could barely speak. "Thank you."

Cope had to lean in to make out the words. "Don't talk. Save your strength."

Now, surprisingly lucid, the man continued to speak in a whisper. "I'm—dying. I know that—It's all right—I'm—ready."

"I'd help if I could."

The voice cleared slightly. "Beyond—help."

"Who did this to you?"

"Chilton—Lawrence—Chilton—shot me."

"Are you Reverend Armitage?"

"—yes...."

Then clarification of this incident became apparent. Cholla—or Chilton, as this man knew him—killed him, possibly to assume his identity. Why else would he take the man's clothes? Likely to go to God's Acres acting as the reverend to pull off some scheme.

"No more talk," Cope said. "I'll stay with you."

Armitage smiled wanly, and closed his eyes. His breathing, though exceedingly shallow, still existed. Cope would remain with him until the end came. Least he could do. He fixated on Cholla's malicious nature and renewed his determination to track down and kill the man before any more innocents were sacrificed for his gains.

Two hours into his vigil, Armitage's breathing became more labored. Lucidity was lost. His pulse became almost nonexistent. It wouldn't be long.

He cursed himself for his inability to help. Trying to make the man more comfortable hadn't worked, and all it did was cause Cope to berate himself further.

Within moments, Armitage was dead. Still, Cope confirmed it. Death had taken this man who should not have died. He *had* to make this right. Cholla would pay and pay dearly for this—for *all* his transgressions. Cope would see to that.

But now, a burial was in order.

He pulled his legs from beneath the body, noticing blood stains on his pants from the head wounds as he stood up. After allowing blood circulation to return to his limbs, he moved to the packhorse to find the necessary instrument. At the side of the trail near the body, he began solemnly digging a shallow grave.

———

DEBORAH STRAWBRIDGE CROSSED THE MAIN STREET of the little town of God's Acres as briskly as she did most everything else in her life. A willowy blonde with delicate features, she was the diametric opposite of the person her appearance presented. Although dressed in a plain gingham dress and sun bonnet and carrying herself gracefully, she had a singleness of purpose that remained hidden until she spoke.

As she reached the mid-point of the crossing, her big green eyes widened, and her pleasant smile changed to a look of concern. She stopped and studied the approach of two horsemen riding slowly toward her. These two again. Her concern transitioned to upset as the riders continued to draw near. Her feet widened into a stance that communicated determination and her hands went to rest on her hips.

The men came to a halt, ten feet away, and removed their big black hats. "Miss Strawbridge."

Deborah stood her ground and refused acknowledgement of the greeting. Not their first visit, but this will be their last.

"I told you Mormons the last time, we have no intention of converting." Her voice was strong and loud and failed to square with her look of refinement. "I also told you to leave and stay away. Yet, here you are, back to make another try."

"We are simply here to offer you the protection of the Mormon brethren. A band of Ute jumped the reservation and are raiding in this area. We can help you."

"We don't need or want your help," Deborah said flatly.

"We have encountered these godless renegades before and have prevailed—"

"As have we!" Deborah's voice increased in volume. "We didn't need help then and we don't need it now. We've done just fine establishing God's Acres as a Baptist stronghold in your Mormon country. I foresee no problem resisting a group of ill equipped savages and I don't need to be beholden to your sect for assistance we neither desire or require. You can leave now and see you don't come back."

"Miss Strawbridge," the man said in protest, "we've been sent by our leaders to—"

"Did you hear the words I just spoke?"

"Yes."

"Then remember them. Go back and tell your leaders what I said." Her next words were measured and precise and very direct. "We don't need you here. Leave us alone!"

The two men glanced at each other. They seemed to realize that further overtures would bear no fruit. They pulled their horses around and started up the street in the direction from which they had come, replacing their hats as they rode. Deborah stood there in the middle of the street until the riders cleared the edge of town. Only then did she relax and continue striding across the street.

Her destination was a structure bearing a sign that identified it as Government Building. She entered quickly and proceeded to a small roll top desk on which papers were strewn. As she seated herself in the desk chair, a light-haired young man stepped away from the single window and approached her. He had a strapping build and wore a Henley type shirt and simple pants supported by dark suspenders. His face was clean shaven and had handsome features coupled with piercing blue eyes.

"What did they want?" His voice was pleasant but agitated.

"Same as usual," she answered without looking up. "This time they offered to protect us from a Ute raiding party they say jumped the reservation. I told them to—"

"Deborah, maybe it wouldn't hurt to accept their help... at least just this one time."

"No, Mason, we can't be beholden to them in any way. They'll use it to force conversion on us. I wish Reverend Armitage would get here soon. At least, if we have a spiritual leader here, that's one less argument they can use against us."

"I agree, but if the Ute attack, we'll need every gun we can get."

"Not at that price. We've defended this place successfully before without their help and we'll do it again. Spread the word about this and make sure everyone is ready for an attack."

"All right. I'll set up some sentries outside of town as well."

"Good."

Mason started for the door. Deborah moved to a rifle rack attached to the wall. He stepped out as she pulled down and checked every weapon in the rack for readiness.

Once this was finished, she returned to the desk. The door opened to admit him once again. This time his expression was animated, almost exhilarated.

"Deborah, come see this."

Curious, she joined him as he returned to the street. He pointed to the east, showing her the approach of a Conestoga wagon driven by a man in a black frock coat and black top hat. The wagon moved slowly, laboriously toward them. Mason became more excited as he spoke.

"Do you suppose that might be—?"

"—Reverend Armitage?" She completed his question.

"Won't be long before we know."

The wagon, driven by Cholla, continued into town. Looking around on both sides of the street to see no one else present, he drove directly to them and pulled back on the reins. "Good day, folks. I'm looking for Miss Deborah Strawbridge."

She responded quickly. "Yes, I'm Deborah."

Noting her reaction, Cholla chose his words carefully and tipped his hat. "Rupert Armitage, Miss Strawbridge. I'm so glad to finally meet you."

Deborah involuntarily clapped her hands in her excitement at his words. "Mr. Armitage, you have no idea how timely your arrival is. Please climb down and come inside."

Cholla wrapped the reins around the brake handle and stepped down from the seat to be met by Deborah's hand, outstretched in greeting. He took the hand in both of his with as much warmth as he could muster and tried to match the smile that was beaming on her face.

"This is Mason Eiling," she nodded toward Mason. "He takes care of our safety."

Cholla exchanged a vigorous handshake with the young man.

"You must be exhausted," Eiling said.

"It has been a long trip," Cholla replied, "but I'm anxious to settle in and get started."

Deborah, seemingly eager as well, asked Eiling to take the wagon and team to the site of the unfinished church and rectory at the end of the street while she showed Cholla into the building from which they had just emerged.

"When you're rested," she told Cholla as they moved, "I'll call a town meeting and introduce you."

She continued speaking as they entered the building. At the same time, Eiling climbed aboard the wagon and started it down the street.

16

NOW CLOSE TO THE UTAH BORDER, an exhausted Cope came upon a tiny cabin nestled in a growth of trees just north of his route. His search for shelter had taken him into this area. This place seemed to present that possibility. Two horses were tethered outside the cabin and smoke rose lazily from its chimney, two signs that the place was inhabited. In great need of rest, he approached openly.

The crack of a rifle shattered the deathly quiet, causing him to draw his mount up sharply. The packhorse sauntered alongside him and stopped. The puff of gun smoke rose above the window from which the shot had emanated. Immediately, a youthful voice called out from inside, "Get gone from here! Don't you come no closer!"

He was a dead-on target out here. He raised his hands to shoulder level and shouted, "I mean you no harm. I'm just a traveler looking to rest a spell."

Silence was his reply, silence that lasted the most of a minute. He stayed in position and offered a further incentive.

"I got food I can share."

More silence. He grew more uncomfortable, wanting now

to forget this idea and continue his search. More movement might draw another, perhaps better aimed shot. He maintained his position.

"You go tie up your animals with the others there and stay out where I can see you," came the order from the young voice.

Obediently, Cope directed his mount and the packhorse to the picket line and proceeded to dismount and follow the directions, staying in full view of the window.

"Now, come on to the door, slow-like."

Abiding by the instructions, Cope stepped slowly toward the door, keeping his hands, palms forward, at shoulder height. The barrel of the rifle poked through the slightly raised window. It followed his movement until he was within two feet of the entrance.

"Door's open," said the voice from inside. "Come on in."

Lifting the latch and pushing gently on the door gained him entrance to the almost minuscule interior. He stepped across the threshold and stopped.

The boy could be no more than fifteen and quite unsure of himself, but his possession of the big .45-70 Remington Rolling Block seemed to do much to bolster his courage. He'll be tall. He's already only a head shorter than me. Light complexioned and blond with long unruly hair that screamed for washing and grooming, the youth wore tattered and nondescript clothes and well-worn shoes. He held the rifle steady—square on Cope's middle.

"If you're going to shoot me, boy, do it now," Cope said, attempting to lighten the mood with levity. "My arms are getting tired."

"He ain't going to shoot you less'n you compel such treatment." These words, spoken in an aged, feeble voice, drew Cope's attention beyond the boy to the figure on the bed against the wall. The cough that followed the statement brought blood to the man's lips, staining the huge white mustache and drooling onto his overgrown beard. He wheezed noticeably.

Cope studied the old man. Folds of flesh hung from his body. At one time, he had been overweight but, due to the illness that obviously afflicted him, he was now no more than skin and bones. The young man transferred his attention to the ailing man, affording Cope the chance to disarm him. He took a pass on the opportunity, though, concentrating more on the old man's condition than his own well-being.

"You don't appear well, old timer. Maybe I can help."

"Don't trouble yourself. Consumption got me. Ain't nothing to do for me." This statement was made haltingly through more coughs and wheezes.

The boy turned back to Cope. "State your business, mister!"

"Got no business, son. I'm just a traveler looking to rest a mite and be on my way."

"Let him in, Huey," the old man said.

"Yes, sir." The boy lowered the hammer of the weapon and directed its aim to the floor planks.

He lowered his hands and stepped further into the cabin. Huey closed the door but held on to the rifle and moved behind Cope as he approached the bed.

"Name's Cope Worley. I don't know doctoring, but I've seen consumption before. I'll do what I can for you, if you'll allow it."

"Obliged to you, stranger, but ain't nothing'll help. I'm that far along." The old man said this through heavier coughing and wheezing, almost complete loss of breath.

Cope removed his coat, balled it up and handed it behind him to Huey. "I'm going to lift him. Put the coat behind his neck."

Silently, the youngster took the coat and set the rifle aside. Cope leaned in and placed a hand beneath each of the old man's shoulders, lifting him away from the meager pillow. Quickly, the youth carried out Cope's directions. Cope then lowered the man to a more upright position. This facilitated the breathing process. Exhausted, the old man trailed off into sleep.

"I'm Huey Ledbetter, Mr. Worley. That there's my uncle, Silas. We be on our way to God's Acres, west of here, in the Utah Territory. Leastways, we was till Uncle Silas got too sick to travel. That's why we holed up here. He wanted me to go on and leave him behind, but I done refused. I won't leave him. I'll wait with him till he can go again."

God's Acres. Coincidence? Perhaps.

He'd just hang onto that for the present. Time enough for digging deeper into that later. For now, he had a far more difficult task to perform.

He sat across from Huey at the tiny, rough-hewn table on the opposite side of the cabin from the bed. A sudden fatherly instinct took hold of him. "You're a good boy, Huey, but I got to tell you, your uncle won't be traveling again. Consumption, at this stage, is a killer. I got no idea how much time he's got left, but it won't be long. I know that much."

"I ain't leaving him."

"I'd never tell you to do that. I'm just preparing you for what's bound to come."

"Mr. Worley, ain't there nothing you can do for to help him?"

"I'd like nothing better, but he's just too far gone."

By the end of that statement, Cope's mind was made up. While it interfered with the immediacy of his mission, seeing this through became the only choice his conscience would allow. "Making him comfortable's all we can do for him now."

"We?"

"I'll be staying on with you, Huey, for as long as it takes. It's hard enough watching a loved one die. No one should be alone with that." Cope's memory of E.J. caused his voice to crack a bit. He had to clear his throat before he could continue.

"He's resting now. I'm going to take care of the horses and see if I can find some more wood for the fire. You sit with him. I won't be long."

—

OVER THE NEXT TWO DAYS, COPE did all he could to keep Silas Ledbetter at ease, constantly refreshing his position to facilitate more effortless breathing and administering broths and gruels he concocted to keep up the man's strength. But, during that time, Silas's condition became progressively worse. At this point, even a doctor couldn't do more.

On the afternoon of the third day, during which Huey attempted to locate and bring down an animal for food, Silas spoke to Cope with great effort. "I am thankful for your efforts, futile as they may be. Might I ask you a great favor?"

"Whatever I can do."

"When I'm gone, if you can see that Huey gets to God's Acres safe, I'd be beholden to you. I have a niece there. She'll take him in, surely."

Silas' voice was but a hoarse whisper, his request interrupted several times by hacking up blood and loss of breath. Fighting through that, he managed to accomplish his purpose.

"Ease yourself." He placed a hand on the man's shoulder. "I'll see the boy safely there. I promise you that."

Silas smiled and nodded, trailing off again from the exhausting struggle of simply speaking. Cope allowed his hand to remain on Silas' shoulder as a comfort.

Huey returned a short time later, his hunt having proven fruitless. Cope offered more of the supplies from his packhorse to sustain them until they found time to replenish.

"Your uncle asked me to see you on to God's Acres."

"I can travel by myself," Huey said. "I'm capable."

"Got no doubt of that, boy, but I promised your uncle I'd see you there safe."

"But I'd be taking you out of your way."

"Huey, I'm not debating this with you. I keep my promises. Besides, I'm heading that way myself. Got some unfinished business there."

Huey glanced across at his uncle and then back to Cope. "How is he?"

The way he asked it, he seemed to already know the answer.

Cope shook his head and scrunched his face in a negative gesture but did not speak. A tear welled in Huey's eye as Cope's actions verified his suspicion. He steeled himself against breaking down and looked back at his uncle.

"Hang on, son. I'm here with you."

Huey stared at Silas for several moments, lost in his thoughts. "He's been ma and pa to me since I was a little shaver. My folks died in a accident. Uncle Silas took me in and raised me like his own. Taught me reading and writing and to cipher some. We was heading to God's Acres to hook up with his niece, Deborah. She's his sister, Lou's, girl. Wanted us to be like a real family. Then he got the sickness worse and couldn't go no more."

"We'll get you there," Cope said. "You'll be a family."

Huey listened to his uncle's labored breathing for several moments longer. "He sounds some better, don't he?"

"Don't let that fool you, Huey. It's only making him comfortable that makes him sound better. It's not helping the damn sickness. 'Fraid nothing can."

In late afternoon, with Huey seated on the side of the bed, the old man opened his eyes and feebly reached his hand to Huey's arm and then removed it. As the hand returned to the bed, his breathing stopped. His eyes closed, and he lay quite still. At this, Cope, at the table, moved to the bed, placing fingers at the jugular area to test for the life that was obviously not there.

"He's gone."

Huey sat there staring at the body of his uncle.

Cope placed his hand on the boy's shoulder. The kid had just lost the only family he'd ever known. "Men cry too, son. Believe me, I know of that."

He watched as the boy allowed the sadness to engulf him and gave himself over to the grief that welled up in him. As he whimpered and sobbed, Cope's hand went behind his neck and drew him close. For several moments, Huey wept uncontrollably. Cope kept a strong hold on him and, slowly, the weeping began to subside.

A few minutes later, when Huey calmed down, Cope lifted the blanket and covered Silas' body completely.

"Sorry for being blunt in your grieving time, but your uncle's got to be buried. Are you up to helping me?"

Huey nodded and rose. Cope led the way outside and fetched a shovel from the items secured to his pack animal. They selected a burial site in the woods near the cabin and took turns digging a shallow grave. Complete darkness covered the area when they finished the project and, before bringing the body to the location, Cope transported a lighted coal oil lamp to mark the spot. Using the blanket from the bed, they wrapped Silas' body and carried it to the opening, placing it carefully within its confines. Cope could not help noticing how little the old man's body weighed.

They stopped long enough to pay silent last respects and then began scooping the loose earth back over the body. In short order, the grave was mounded over. Exhausted, they walked slowly back to the cabin where Cope spent a restless night attempting to sleep and Huey, having broken off a floor plank, fashioned a grave marker using a hunting knife to carve out Silas's name. Then, totally spent, Huey finally succumbed to sleep.

In the morning, Cope awakened early and noted that Huey was sleeping peacefully. The poor kid had run out of goods. Cope allowed him to rest for as long as he needed. Easing himself outside, he cared for the horses and used the shovel to pound the grave marker into place. Then he made the necessary arrangements to facilitate their journey to God's Acres, checking the pack animal's rigging and saddling the Ledbetter horses. After that, he prepared a quick but substantial meal for them both. The food was waiting for Huey when the boy rose several hours later.

He thanked Cope for his kindnesses, although very little conversation went on between the two.

They finished the meal and Huey took a few moments alone at the gravesite to bid his uncle a final farewell. From the picket line, Cope watched him fight back the tears of sadness and loss. While Cope made the horses ready for travel, Huey returned to the cabin and emerged a few seconds later appearing to adjust something inside his coat. Cope discounted this as anything important. With the unoccupied saddle horse in tow, they struck out for God's Acres.

———

TWO DAYS INTO THE JOURNEY, HUEY began exhibiting an uneasy feeling. He continually and noticeably checked the path behind them. After a few of these incidents, Cope brought it up.

"What's wrong? You're acting like you're being chased."

"I, eh, I ain't exactly sure, Mr. Worley. Something just feels off, like we're not alone out here."

"Animals, maybe?"

"Maybe. Or might could be the two-legged kind."

"Likely nothing but can't hurt to keep a closer watch." Cope's hand went to rest on the butt of his revolver. Huey renewed his hold on the big Remington resting at the ready across his saddle. They continued to ride.

Memories of being stalked during his law enforcement encounters returned to Cope. His suspicion rose that more was going on here than met the eye.

"Huey, is there anything you want to tell me? You know, I am trying to help you."

"I know that, but, no—no, there's nothing."

There was something. He'd bet on it. The kid just wasn't letting on to it. What was it and how could he get it out of him?

"There's somebody back there," Huey said, breaking his train of thought.

He joined Huey in looking around. A lone horseman sat his saddle back in the distance.

"That ain't good," Huey said.

"Could be just another traveler, but we're not going to take any chances."

They whipped up the horses and upped their speed to close to a gallop in an attempt to put distance between them and the rider. In doing so, they allowed their attention to concentrate on riding and not on the happenings around them.

The gunshot changed that abruptly. Immediately following the sound, a figure stepped out from behind bushes in front of them under the cloud of rising gun smoke. They hastily reined in as they spotted the revolver in his hand. The packhorse and the extra animal did not obey as quickly as did their own mounts, placing the animals in the center of a chaotic situation.

"Stay where you be! I got you covered!" The voice of the figure snarled in a thick Southern accent.

Involved in bringing the horses to heel without losing

control of them, neither Cope nor Huey had the opportunity to put weapons into play.

"Hands up!"

Disadvantaged, they complied as Huey's Remington slipped from the saddle, landing in the dirt beside his horse.

The intruder took a step forward.

"All right, light down from there."

17

HE WAS A BIG MAN WEARING non-descript, ragged clothes and a filthy *kepi*—the round flat-topped gray cap that had been Confederate infantry issue back during the war. The hat had a worn, grimy visor. His face was long with a kind of round mouth framed by a massive mustache that reached down the sides of his mouth almost to his jaw line. In his hand, a .44 caliber percussion revolver waived ominously.

Cope and the boy remained silent after dismounting and stood with hands at shoulder level. They stepped away from the animals as ordered. The man said nothing more, but kept the weapon trained on his captives, relieving Cope of his revolver and heaving the gun behind him onto the road.

During this short interval, the horseman on the trail behind them had increased his speed and, now at full gallop, headed straight for them. The man with the gun periodically looked in the rider's direction, obviously awaiting his arrival.

An expert rider, the man on the horse thundered in and pulled rein, dropping quickly from the saddle. Not as tall as his cohort, this man had a round, smiling face that sported a pure white, unkempt mustache that matched the shock of thick white hair peeking out in disarray from under his wide-brimmed, straw hat. His clothes were as shabby as his companion's, and he wore his knee-length boots over his trouser legs.

"Hey, Brittles, good job." He joined the big man and produced and cocked his own handgun.

"Yeah, I knew my idee'd work," Brittles replied.

The white-haired man approached Huey, ignoring Cope. Brittles stepped behind Cope and cuffed him across the back of his hat with the barrel of the revolver. Cope yelped at the hit and sank to a pile where he had stood. While not unconscious, he was rendered momentarily senseless, enough to take him out of the fray. He could only take in what happened next.

"You be old man Ledbetter's nephew, ain't you?" the white-haired man addressed Huey.

"Yeah," Huey replied tentatively.

"You know who we be?"

"No, I don't."

"My name's Lasky. His be Brittles." He poked the boy in the chest. "Your uncle owes us money."

"Yeah," Brittles added, "money he done swindled us out of."

Huey remained silent, but grew agitated at the accusation.

"Now, we done found where at you was staying," Lasky continued, "and we done found Silas's grave. We done turned that cabin upside up and down again. And we ain't found no money. That makes us think maybe you got it. How about that, kid?"

"I don't know nothing about no money," Huey protested. "Uncle Silas weren't no swindler."

"We done followed y'all clear from way back home," Lasky said, "We ain't leaving without we gets what's our'n."

Suddenly, Huey seemed to find courage to take a stand against overwhelming odds. "No, Uncle Silas got that money fair and square. He told me about you two—how you tried to get his money. That's why we kept it hid. He told me not to tell no one about it and I didn't."

"That's all well and good, sonny," Lasky told him, "but the money's our'n. We wants it now."

Cope, now coming back to a point at which he could do more than observe, opened his eyes to assess his situation. Lasky stood close to Huey with Brittles standing equally distant between them and Cope. Damn it, his gun was too far away. No help there. He had to do this quick, on the fly and unarmed.

He waited without moving.

"Search the kid," Brittles said.

Lasky stepped closer and reached out to conduct a search of the boy's clothes. Brittles came closer in anticipation of the result. With a sudden move, Huey grabbed Lasky's hand and shoved the man away. The grappling that followed forced Lasky's weapon into Huey's midsection. There was a shot and Huey screamed and crumpled, then slumped to the ground. Drawn to the scuffle and the shot, Brittles made the mistake of looking away from Cope.

Now!

Pulling his legs swiftly under him, Cope sprang at the two men with his arms spread wide to form a scoop. He connected solidly, his right arm and shoulder colliding with Lasky while his left arm shoved the off-balance Brittles to the side. As Brittles' body slammed to the ground, he took Lasky to a similar position. Instantly, he grabbed for the revolver in Lasky's hand and ripped it free. Brittles rolled onto his back and swung his weapon into play. Cope glanced that way, but couldn't get a shot off in time. He lifted Lasky by the shirt slightly off the ground, using the man's body as a shield.

A round belched from the gun and found its mark in Lasky's back. The older man screamed in pain at the entry of the bullet. Cope watched as the slug exited Lasky's chest, spewing blood and body matter all over him. Lasky's body went limp.

Brittles sat there dumbstruck by the result of his action.

Cope let go of Lasky's body and swung the gun over it, laying a bead on Brittles. Without hesitation, he cocked the piece and fired a round into his attacker's shoulder. The hit threw Brittles back onto the ground. Almost in one movement, Cope shoved Lasky's away and came to his feet. He stepped over the corpse and converged on Brittles. He put his weight on Brittles' wrist with one foot and kicked the gun away with the other. His wound wouldn't kill him, but it was bad enough so he couldn't fight.

He turned and hurried back to Huey, assessing the boy's condition as he knelt beside him. Just barely breathing. He pulled Huey's shirt away to reveal the wound—square in the belly. Heavy bleeding. That size ball, that close... he was done for.

He put his hand behind the boy's head in a futile effort to comfort him.

Huey opened his eyes and focused on Cope. "Am I shot? Did he shoot me?"

"Yeah, Huey," Cope's voice broke giving the answer. "He did."

"Am—am I going to die?"

He couldn't tell him true. Not right. Served no purpose. "No, boy, you'll be fine. You just lay still now. You need to rest."

Huey closed his eyes and attempted to follow instructions. His labored breathing became weaker as the moments progressed, and before long, it stopped completely.

Cope made the obligatory check for a pulse.

Shit! What a waste.

As he laid the boy flat, his hand passed a lump in Huey's coat. He reached in and turned up the package Huey had secreted there, opened it to find money inside. Without bothering to count the currency, he set it beside the body and looked at Huey's face.

It was his fault the boy was dead. He should have moved

quicker, sooner. His task at hand right now, bury the boy the best way possible. This would be his last act of kindness for Huey who had harkened to his uncle's instructions and fought valiantly to defend his belief in the honesty of the man who raised him. After that, find his relative in God's Acre. Tell the story and deliver the money.

Right now, there was something else—that son of a bitch over there. Time to resolve this.

He rose and walked purposefully to the point at which his gun had landed. Retrieving it, he turned and approached Brittles who lay languishing in the pain of his wound.

"Hey, you! That old man didn't swindle you, did he?"

Brittles didn't answer.

"I asked you a question!" Cope said in a loud, commanding voice, "I want an answer!"

"I'm hurt."

He leaned in. "I don't give a damn. Answer me. Did the old man swindle you?"

"Naw! He come by it honest-like. Lasky and me, we tried at swindling him but he seed through it and run off with the kid. So, we followed them. Too much money to let it go."

Well, that was cleared up, but to no satisfaction. It vindicated Silas and Huey, but did not excuse the conduct of these two sidewinders.

Overwhelming anger seized Cope, almost equaling what he experienced at E.J.'s death. He couldn't just leave this hanging.

"Your partner's dead. Give me one good reason why I shouldn't send you to hell with him."

Brittles' expression was one of wonderment. Pain likely clouding his thinking but, deep down, maybe he doesn't believe I'll do it. His response came out weak and carried no conviction. "I'm sorry?"

"Not good enough." He cocked the Colt and, without

hesitation, placed one vengeful shot in the man's heart, killing him instantly.

———

COPE BURIED HUEY ON THE SIDE of the road in much the same manner as Reverend Armitage and with just as much solemnity and care. He took the time, as he had done with the minister, to carve a headstone from a stout limb. The least he could do.

In his final act of vindictiveness toward Lasky and Brittles, he dragged their bodies into the brush and heaped them together to rot there. They deserved no better. Dragging them away was no more than clearing the trail. Their journey to hell would not be marked by even the protection of some scratched over dirt.

After collecting all the horses—including the intruders'—he prepared to set out again for God's Acres. As his last action prior to leaving, he scribbled out a cursory note on a slip of paper he placed in his saddlebag. He took with him, in addition to several more weapons, the hidden money, Huey's name and the name of Huey's relative, Deborah. He would seek her out and inform her of the Ledbetter's fate and pass on the funds.

Then Cholla.

Stoically, resolutely, he moved on.

A settlement just inside the Utah border afforded him the opportunity to sell off the extra horses and guns. These gains he added to Huey's stash, with the exception of a few dollars used to replenish his supplies and to replace his dirt encrusted clothes. Verification of his route to God's Acres met with difficulty since he found himself in a Mormon village. The elders frowned on what they termed the foreign religion practiced there and refused to cooperate with Cope. Using force of will and a little corporal persuasion, Cope prevailed and confirmed that continuing due west would bring him to God's Acres inside a week. He rode on.

———

IN THE PARTIALLY COMPLETED CHURCH, CHOLLA stood alone. It had been two days since his arrival. Now, well-fed and rested, thanks in large part to Deborah Strawbridge, he resided in a small room in the government building instead of the wagon. This afforded not only privacy, but warmth and a modicum of comfort. Continuing to play the role of the minister, he ventured out to the church to examine the mechanism which he would use to bilk this unsuspecting flock before moving on. Several ideas came to mind, all of which he kept for further consideration.

Deborah entered the building as Cholla studied the simplicity of the lectern that stood in the center of the raised platform that formed the altar. Makeshift benches filled the room. An aisle the width of two people ran down the center. The clapboard walls had many cutouts for windows yet to be installed. Above them, the roof was a work in progress, unfinished in several spots.

"What do you think of it so far?" she asked as she approached.

Cholla looked around as if deeply interested. "I'm impressed. It's as if every person here contributed something."

She smiled back. "They did. This was done by loving hands."

"I can tell," he said. "I can see it."

"I can't tell you how happy I—*we* are to finally have you here. This will make all our work complete. When the church is finished, and you conduct our first service, it will be the culmination of everything my parents and I, and every person here, have worked so hard for."

He picked up on her anticipation and played into it. "Now, Deborah, there's no need to wait until the church is finished. This is merely an enclosure, a meeting place. There is no reason why we can't have our first service this Sunday. Shall we say, ten o'clock?"

Deborah's face lit up. "You're right. I'll spread the word. Everyone will come. It will be like one big family."

"Absolutely."

18

COPE CONTINUED WEST, PRESSING HIS ANIMALS as hard as he did himself, stopping only when absolutely necessary for food and water. Seldom did he rest, and he provided none of the same for his horses.

The outline of the buildings that made up God's Acres were visible from about a mile out. Moving out of the mountainous terrain of Colorado and onto the flatter plains of Utah afforded him a long-distance view of the land ahead of him. Previously gleaned information convinced him this landscape was his ultimate destination. He drew rein at that spot and reached for his spy-glass amid the various goods residing in his saddlebags. It took some probing, but he located it.

After adjusting the instrument in, he scanned the rooftops and zeroed in on the steeple of the church building, made apparent by the cross affixed to its tip. Assuming his assessment of Cholla's previous actions were correct, he would pass himself off as Reverend Armitage to the people of God's Acres. Cholla's reasons for doing this escaped Cope and, truth be told, held little interest to him save for the fact that some ulterior motive had to be at the heart of it.

Cholla had at least a week to settle in here and had likely gained their trust by now. This could have a bearing on the success of Cope's mission. Riding openly into the town and announcing his intentions would surely be met with resistance and would warn Cholla off. In this case, subterfuge and obscurity should be his methods. Slowly and carefully, he resumed his ride toward the town, keeping as low a profile as possible.

In order to gain as much strategic information as he could about God's Acres, he skirted the town in a wide circle. This gave him a picture, though somewhat distant, of the layout.

The church is at the end of town closest to me. It's set apart from the rest of the buildings by about an eighth of a mile. Beside it, a small tri-walled stable. Behind the stable, there's the Conestoga wagon, unhitched from its team. Likely the wagon driven by Reverend Armitage. Verifying the loads in his revolver and returning the cylinder to the customary empty chamber under the hammer, he approached the scene with stealth. Dismounting and tying his horses off in the bushes a short distance away, he proceeded on foot.

Arriving at the wagon, he made certain no one was around and then proceeded to climb over the tailgate and into the back. A quick reconnoiter of the inside confirmed this to be indeed Reverend Armitage's possession. Clothing and personal articles obviously belonged to the minister. The prospect of it being a different cleric was remote enough to discount. Satisfied to this point, he climbed back down and proceeded into the animal enclosure.

Several horses were quartered there, but one, in particular, stood out to Cope. The white mare, because of her color and bearing, definitely the same animal E.J. had sold to Cholla. About a year older, but, without a doubt, the same one. God, that seems so long ago! He let his mind wander back to E.J. and he dwelled there for a few seconds that gave the impression of being much longer. But the digression was short lived. He was this close to confronting Cholla. That needs a clear head.

Exiting, he moved carefully to the rear of the church and stopped at the single window that was next to the entry door. Removing his hat, he leaned closer to the pane for a look inside.

A small room about half the width of the actual building. A table and chair there and not much more. Maybe a preparation room provided for the minister to craft his sermons and to make ready for his services. A door in the far corner likely led into the church itself. The other half of the back of the structure might be devoted to tools or supplies, based on the fact that the door to this enclosure was padlocked. But the most motivating sight, the man in the black frock coat seated at the table with his back to the window. Got to be Cholla. Cope took a second to calm his anticipation. This has to be done safely and intelligently. Surprise him. He lifted his sidearm from its holster and held it along his leg pointed at the ground.

The back door was unsecured. Cope's left hand turned the knob and pushed. The door swung open, remarkably making not a sound. A rush of fresh air caressed Cholla's neck. If he picked up on that, it came too late as Cope stepped into the room and leveled the revolver.

"Cholla! Get up. Turn around."

Cope's voice was deep, even and ominous. Cholla froze. Likely already trying to figure a way out of this.

Cope took a step closer. "Do what I told you!"

Cholla raised his hands. "What do you want?"

"You," Cope said curtly, "now, get up!"

Reluctantly, Cholla rose. The chair upended behind him and fell to its back on the wood plank floor. He did not turn. Cope stepped in and kicked the chair away. It slid noisily to a corner of the room. Cope reached his left hand to Cholla's left arm and yanked him around. Off balance, Cholla swung against the table and caught himself to prevent falling. Recognition registered on his face as he gazed at Cope.

"*Worley!*"

"Right, you son of a bitch. Worley. I been trailing you the better part of a year and now you're mine. You took her from me and now you're going to pay."

Cope read the thoughts behind those eyes. The bank. The shooting. Worley's wife—It was Worley's *wife*. He'd likely figured it was her all along, but now he was certain.

Now, his face showed his realization of Cope's intention, but he remained strangely calm. "She got in the way."

"You shot her down like a dog for no reason."

Cholla's voice was one of quiet reason. "I was aiming at the teller. She got in the way."

"That's all this means to you?" Cope said, "She got in the way? She was my *wife!* You took her from me and you're telling me, she got in the way?"

Cholla did not reply.

Rage consumed Cope, not only for the fact that he was confronting the man who killed E.J., but for the cavalier attitude the man took. No contrition, not even any remorse, just clinging to the fact that she got in the way. Cope lost it! His left fist struck out in a swift jab that caught Cholla's jaw and propelled him and the table across the room. The table landed on its side. Cholla wound up, his mouth leaking blood, over the table and on his back on the floor.

Cope stepped forward and shoved a boot against the table to clear his way. As the table slid away, Cholla scrambled to his feet, but apparent pain from the wound and loss of wind from the fall caused him to falter. Cope switched the gun to his left hand and stepped into a right cross that scraped Cholla's chin and sent him slamming into the door leading into the church. Latch and hinges sagged under the force and weight of Cholla's body. The door flew aside, allowing Cholla to plummet onto the floor of the altar. He landed hard on his arm and side, obviously experiencing more pain and injuries.

His initial anger now spent to the point of being able to again regain reason, Cope stepped through the opening as Cholla rolled to his back and attempted to get up.

"Stay down, you son of a bitch!" Cope said, "Stay down! Just don't. Don't you move or, I swear to God, I'll kill you right here—right now!"

"What the hell, you're going to kill me, anyway."

"That was my intent. I'll give you that. I was going to beat you senseless and then take whatever's left of you just like you took E.J. But no, that's too easy, too fast. I'm taking you back to hang. You got that, Cholla? You're going to hang for killing E.J. and all the others you ended. And I'm going to enjoy the hell out of watching it."

Cholla glanced around frantically. Trying to figure a plan, no doubt. He glared at Cope. "You don't have the guts to pull that trigger."

Cope shifted the revolver to his right hand and cocked the piece. "Cholla, you don't know me or what I've become. Or what I can do. Your partners, the ones still alive, they know. They can attest to that. So just you stay down, you hear me? Or you'll find out exactly what I'm capable of."

"Hold it."

The third voice came from behind Cope. Uncertain of the intentions of this stranger, he froze in place. "Drop that gun."

"You don't savvy," Cope said. He had to try.

"I savvy what I see. You, holding a gun on the minister. Now drop it or I'll cut you in half."

Any hope of Cope controlling this situation slipped away when the stranger placed the rifle barrel against his back. No one had the ability to outmaneuver a bullet. Allowing the hammer to ease down to rest, Cope let the gun rock forward on his trigger finger.

"Let it go!"

Cope let the piece drop to the floor. It made a loud thud. As he raised his hands to shoulder level, the stranger came around him. Young, good looking, pretty confident. No chance to turn it on him.

"Are you all right, Reverend?" the man asked, keeping his eyes squarely on Cope.

Cholla nodded. "Yes, Mason. Just get him away from me."

"What's this all about?"

"I don't know," Cholla replied, "Just, please, remove him."

Mason Eiling pushed Cope backward with the barrel of the rifle and snatched up the revolver from the floor.

"You heard him," Eiling inserted the weapon in his waistband, "Out."

Cope moved slowly toward the back door. Eiling fell in behind and followed him out.

Cholla remained in place until they were out of sight, then got to his feet and bolted out and over to the wagon. Climbing inside, he immediately uncovered from its hiding place the Colt New Line revolver and its shoulder holster. Hastily stripping off his coat, he slipped into the rig and checked the weapon's loads. Satisfied, he scratched out extra cartridges and dropped them into a coat pocket before pulling the garment back on.

Peering through the window of the government building, Deborah Strawbridge caught sight of Eiling marching a stranger down the center of the street. The man had his hands at a submissive shoulder level and Eiling walked a few paces behind him, his rifle trained on the man's back. Concerned, she exited the building and hurried toward them.

"Mason," she said as she approached. "What's going on? Who is this?"

Deborah's trajectory intersected with Cope's, causing him to stop. Eiling halted an appropriate distance behind him.

"I don't rightly know," Eiling replied. "He knocked Reverend Armitage down. When I got to the church, he was holding a gun on him. I'm taking him down to the stable to tie him up before I question him."

Deborah stopped. "Is Mr. Armitage all right?"

Eiling shurgged. "He says he is, but I don't know. Looks like he took a pretty bad beating."

"I'll check on him. You go ahead—"

"He's not who he says he is," Cope said.

"What?"

"Your reverend. He's not that. Not at all."

Eiling took a step closer to Cope. "You shut up, mister. I'll tell you when you can talk."

Now, fully invested in this, Deborah took command. "See he's tied up while I see to Mr. Armitage. I'll be along after that. I want to know what this is all about."

Eiling nodded. "Get to moving, you."

Unable to do anything but the kid's bidding, Cope moved forward with Eiling trailing behind as Deborah hurried in the opposite direction toward the church.

Entering through the front doors, she took in the sight of the door to the sanctuary on the floor in the spot it had landed. Serious concern took hold. She moved forward to examine the scene and then proceeded into the room. The table was upended and the back door wide open. No sign of Reverend Armitage. She stepped through the room quickly and looked around outside. No trace of the minister. Now, almost in panic stage, she hiked her dress above her ankles and ran around the side of the building. She proceeded through the street toward

Eiling's destination, the town's livery stable. As she approached, he herded his prisoner inside. Intent on questioning the man, she moved faster.

The interior of the stable was typically laid out, with several horse stalls, some of which were occupied. A wide center space containing tack, feed and the like became the destination for Eiling and his prisoner. He stayed a respectable distance from Cope as Deborah entered.

"How's Reverend Armitage?" He kept his eyes and his gun trained on Cope.

"I don't know. I couldn't find him."

"More'n likely he just ran," Cope said.

She eyed him doubtfully. "Just who are you and what have you got to do with Mr. Armitage?"

"Deborah, he ought to be tied up before we talk to him."

"I'll do it." She fetched a coil of rope from a hook. "You watch him close."

Stepping behind Cope, she pulled his hands behind his back and secured them with the rope.

She moved around to face him. "Now, who are you?"

"Name's Cope Worley. I've spent most of a year tracking that son of—pardon, ma'am. Tracking that man down. He's not your Reverend Armitage. His name's Lorenzo Cholla. I found the reverend on the trail, dying, where Cholla left him. He told me Cholla was his killer before he passed."

Deborah pondered this for a second before speaking. "Granting what you say is true and, mind you, I'm not convinced, why are you chasing him?"

"He killed my wife during a bank robbery he pulled. I took care of the ones with him. He's the last of them."

Deborah showed her resolve faltering, but still she tried to hold to it. "Convince me."

"Wish I could. I had a wanted poster with his likeness on

it, but that's lost. All you got is my word unless you can contact Sheriff Rud Tanner in Senado Pass. He'll vouch for me."

"We have no way of doing that quickly."

"No offense, ma'am, but I need to talk to somebody in authority here."

"You are, Mr. Worley. I'm Deborah Strawbridge, the mayor of God's Acres."

The name *Deborah* flashed through his memory and struck a responsive chord. "Your name being Deborah, ma'am, any of your relatives got the name Ledbetter?"

"Yes. I have several with that name. How do you know about that?"

"Reverend Armitage wasn't the only one I found on the trail. A short time after that, I came across Silas Ledbetter and his nephew, Huey. Said they were headed here. Silas, he was bad sick with the consumption and, I'm sorry to tell you, he died close to a week or so after I met them. Before he passed, he asked me to see Huey here safe and I promised him that. But we got jumped on the trail and, well, Huey didn't make it. He had some money with him. I brought it along with me case I ran in to you. It's in my saddlebag out behind the church."

In that split second, Deborah went from confident to completely shaken by this news. She stared into space for a long moment before requesting more information. "How? How did Huey die?" she asked through a voice cracking with emotion.

"Thieves shot him. He died from his wound. It pains me, I couldn't help him."

Deborah paced, obviously mulling not only this information but the possibility that Worley might be correct about the minister.

"Ma'am," Cope said, "you got to let me loose so I can stop Cholla before he kills again."

"No. I've got to talk to him first."

She turned sharply and strode out of the stable.

"You're making a mistake, ma'am," Cope called after her. "Don't trust him!"

19

SIT YOU DOWN ON THAT BARREL." Eiling pointed with the barrel of his gun.

Making a face that displayed discomfort, he removed Cope's revolver from his waistband and hung it on a nail by the trigger guard. But the rifle in his hands bade Cope to obey. Taking a step back, Cope half sat on the barrel behind him. *If Cholla has the chance to get away, the hunt starts all over again. Can't let that happen, not this close to ending it.* He continued his argument.

"Son, I know you think holding me's the right thing to do, but I'm talking true here. If Cholla's not stopped, he's going to kill anyone gets in his way. Let me go. I can take him."

Eiling's resolve was not shaken. "Not till Deborah says so. She's in charge. You're staying right here."

Cope tried again, taking a different approach. "If you have a care for her at all, don't let her talk to him alone. Go after her. I'm tied. I can't cause any trouble like this."

Eiling's eyes and expression betrayed a slight wavering of determination. "She can take care of herself."

Cope pressed on.

"I'm telling you, Cholla's a killer. Even if you don't believe that, is it worth putting her life at risk? If he harms her, that's on you. Can you live with that?"

Eiling stopped to think on that. Cope waited as the wheels in the man's head turned, watching his eyes. After a moment, understanding seemed to dawn.

He turned quickly and hurried out of the stable.

Cope immediately began working to loosen his bonds, which he had already determined were not as secure as his captors believed.

———

CHOLLA LED THE SADDLED WHITE MARE and another mount behind the street, stopping at the back door to the government building. There he secured the horses and rounded the corner to approach the street, intending to survey present conditions.

The slight breeze that had prevailed during the morning had picked up as the noon hour drew near, culminating now as a steady wind which unseated tumbleweeds from their resting places and raised swirling dust clouds.

Deborah Strawbridge strode determinedly in the center of an empty street toward him. Good. Saved him the trouble of finding her. He pressed himself against the wall of the building and waited for her to come closer.

As she reached the building, instead of turning to enter, she continued toward the church. She walked fast with a determined gait and a look of concern on her face.

Cholla reached inside his coat and brought his revolver to bear. He waited until Deborah moved slightly past the corner.

"Deborah!" He stepped out to intercept her, the gun concealed at his side.

She stopped abruptly and turned toward the voice. "Mr. Armitage, I've been looking for you."

"And I you."

It was then that she noticed the weapon. She shrank back as he brought it up level and held it on her. "What—"

"Do exactly as I say, and you won't be harmed."

Deborah took a second to digest this. "Then it's true what Worley says?"

Her words came out knowing but still incredulous.

"Never mind that," Cholla said. "Get inside. You're going to come in handy."

With no choice, she moved toward the building door as he fell in behind her. She opened the door. He shoved her completely inside and followed, closing the door behind him. She stumbled from the push but caught herself before falling.

"Sit down," he said, pointing to the desk chair.

She complied quietly. He moved to the single window and peered out, deep in thought. Several factors needed to come together to progress his plan and he had to think it through, to plot out the details. Then an image in the street provided the assistance he required.

Mason Eiling strode toward the building quickly, obviously intending to enter. Cholla moved to the wall beside the door and waited.

"You just sit there," he said to Deborah in a harsh whisper. "Don't make a sound."

The door opened to admit Eiling. At first sight he read the alarm on Deborah's face. His reaction time was not fast enough as Cholla kicked the door shut.

"Drop the rifle!" he growled.

Eiling froze.

"Mason—"

Cholla shouted over her. "I said drop it!"

Deborah nodded her head to indicate he had no choice. He let the gun slip from his hands. As it clattered on the floor, Cholla shoved Eiling toward the desk and kicked the Winchester to the side. Mason caught himself on the edge of the desk.

"You're just in time, Mason," Cholla said.

Eiling turned sharply to face Cholla. "If you hurt her...."

"You're not in a position to make threats. In case you didn't notice, I'm in charge here. You'll do as I tell you."

Eiling stood down in complete compliance.

"What do you want?" Deborah asked.

"Two things." Cholla had confidence now that he controlled the situation. "I want Worley. He's dogged me long enough. Time for him to end. Then, I want every dollar this town owns brought to me here. And you, Mason, are my messenger. You'll make this all happen, or it won't go well for Deborah. Do you understand?"

Eiling failed to answer. Cholla's face grew red. He scowled. With a voice of icy malice he repeated the question loudly and precisely. "Do. You. *Understand?*"

Resigned to the fact that they were at bay and at the mercy of this man, Eiling replied, "Yes."

"Good. Now bring Worley here and do it fast."

Eiling looked to Deborah. Her expression told him he had no choice but to comply. Moving to the door, he let himself out. Cholla closed the door and trained his gun on Deborah.

———

IMMEDIATELY AFTER EILING LEFT THE STABLE, Cope labored furiously on the ropes binding him. Deborah's apparent unfamiliarity with knots worked in his favor. Once he eased the tightness, he worked the haphazard knot loose and released his wrists. Pulling the rest of the cords from his hands, he pushed himself up and went directly to the post on which his revolver was suspended. He grabbed the gun and shoved it in his holster as he made for the door. Stopping for a second, he surveyed the street before him. No one in the way. This allowed him access to the street. He crossed on the run and ducked into a narrow alley that led to the area behind the row of buildings. His destination, while keeping out of sight, the church—his objective, Cholla.

As he moved carefully, he came upon two horses secured in back of a building. This is where Deborah governs the town. Again, the white mare stood out, both in Cope's sight and his memory. His mind worked quickly. Cholla was inside. If he was not alone, whoever was in there with him was in danger. In either case, Cope would enter and see this through. One thing needed to be done first.

Reaching the mounts, Cope loosed their reins and led them away from their mooring. He brought them several buildings away, retracing his own steps, at which point he led them into an alley and tied them off. That should throw a crimp into Cholla's plan.

He returned to the government building. There were no windows in the rear. In order to scout the inside, he moved through the alley to the street to make use of the one window he recalled seeing in the front. The wind created enough noise to cover any sound his footsteps made, but he attempted to keep that to a minimum all the same. Stopping at the window, he removed his hat and peered inside while attempting to stay hidden. The angle was not the greatest, but he got enough of the image inside to figure it out. Cholla paced in front of a seated Deborah, his gun trained on her. Got to come up with a plan to disable Cholla while keeping Deborah safe. Nothing immediately came to mind.

"Worley!"

Mason's voice. Not hard to identify even though he kept it muffled into a harsh whisper. Cope whirled with his gun drawn. At this sight, Eiling, in the street, but close to the walkway, stopped and raised his hands.

"I need your help," Eiling said, still in a whisper.

He motioned for Cope to join him in the alleyway, away from the window and Cholla's sight.

Cope complied, keeping him covered.

"Look, I know what you told us is true," Eiling said quietly. "That animal's got Deborah captive in there right now."

"I saw that."

"He wants every cent this town's got, but he wants to kill you first. He sent me out to bring you in. He said he'd kill her if I didn't."

"Then that's our way in."

"Didn't you hear the part about him killing you?"

"I heard it. I can use it. Look, we've got to get inside if we're going to help her. This is the way. You'll take me to him. I'll take it from there."

Eiling wasn't convinced. "What if he just shoots you down when you walk in? How does that help her?"

"I'm gambling he won't. His ego's too big. He'll want to gloat some first. That'll buy time."

"Time for what?"

"Something. Anything. I don't know. I'm ciphering this as it goes." As Cope finished his statement, he allowed the revolver to rotate backward and turned it butt first, handing it to Eiling. Hesitantly, the younger man took the piece.

"Take me to him," Cope said. "Make it look good."

He turned his back to Eiling and raised his hands. Eiling took the hint and trained the gun on Cope as he moved toward the street.

Cholla turned his attention sharply away from Deborah as

the door opened to admit Cope, hands raised, followed closely by Eiling. A smirk crossed Cholla's face.

"Come in, Worley. Welcome."

Cope stepped in. Eiling followed and stepped to the side.

"Drop the gun," Cholla ordered Eiling, turning his revolver back to Deborah to make his point.

Eiling dutifully let the weapon fall and raised his hands. Cope's eyes followed it to its landing position, then moved on to where Eiling's rifle rested. At the same moment, he stepped to the side, creating distance between Cholla and Deborah, putting Cholla in the center. Cholla's eyes followed Cope. His gun remained trained on Deborah.

"Any move you make will result in her death."

"I'm told you want to kill me," Cope continuing to move to the side. "Well, I'm right here. What are you waiting for?"

Cholla grinned as he turned his weapon toward Cope. "I'm in no hurry, Worley, no hurry at all."

His ego was taking hold. Just what they needed.

"You ought to be. You ought to want me gone right quick 'cause, given the chance, I'll kill you, without a second thought."

Deborah's expression betrayed her understanding of Cope's intention, to bait Cholla into making a mistake. Eiling's face already had that knowing look as he shot a glance at Deborah. They seemed to be of the same mind. Then Deborah took the initiative. She came to her feet, allowing the chair to fall noisily behind her.

His attention pulled from Cope, Cholla turned toward the sound. At that instant, Eiling kicked Cope's revolver toward him. Cope stooped as the gun slid toward him, scooping it up. In reaction to the movement, Cholla swung his weapon back toward Eiling and fired, almost blindly. The bullet gouged into the meat of Eiling's left leg, forcing him against the wall. At that moment, Cope snapped off a shot without aiming that chipped a piece of flesh from Cholla's upper right arm. Pushed sideways, he returned fire, wounding Cope in the left shoulder.

Though badly hit, Cope's determination kicked in. The entry of the bullet had folded him initially, but he righted himself and fired back at Cholla. Missing its mark, the slug came close enough to upset Cholla. As Eiling faltered, he attempted to extricate himself from this predicament.

Spinning sharply, Cholla made for the back door as Eiling slumped to the floor. Closest to Eiling, Deborah hurried to him. He waved her off, his hand indicating his wound was not life threatening. She turned her attention to Cope who struggled to remain standing.

Cholla flung the back door open and bolted through the doorway as Deborah reached Cope.

"Get out of here!" Cope said as he pulled himself erect.

"But—"

"Get to safety! Cholla's mine!"

Cholla cleared the door frame. Finding the horses gone, he instantly shifted direction, toward the church stable. He broke into a run, heading for the church as the wind stung his face.

Seconds passed. Cope stepped out the door as Cholla reached the church building and headed down the side toward the stable. Filled with determination to end this, Cope moved forward, trying to ignore the pain in his shoulder.

At the same time, Deborah picked up Eiling's rifle from the floor and made for the front door.

"Deborah, don't!" Eiling shouted through his pain.

Ignoring him, she went through the front door and headed for the church.

Cholla reached the stable and the wagon horses inside. Cope reached the corner of the church and spotted Cholla. His way out. Raising his revolver, Cope fired his remaining three rounds, but checked his aim high enough to avoid hitting the horses. Cholla, unable to get to the horses, whirled and made for the back of the church, ducking inside. Cope, ejecting empty shells and reloading on the run, continued to the door and cautiously opened it. Having reached the door from the office to the church, Cholla turned at the noise of the back door opening and snapped off a shot aimlessly at the sound. The round took a chunk of wood from the door frame close to Cope's head, forcing him away from the door. Responding, Cope pumped two shots into the interior of the building, intending to dislodge Cholla from cover and to interrupt his concentration. This sent Cholla running up the center aisle of the church toward the front door. Boldly, Cope ducked inside and proceeded into the church as Cholla exited the front.

Deborah, approaching the church carefully, watched Cholla emerge and called to him. "Stop!"

Cholla reacted by turning quickly at a right angle and running toward buildings on the opposite side of the street. Deborah shouldered the Winchester, cocked it and pulled the trigger. The hammer fell on an empty chamber, giving Cholla time to reach the buildings and scoot into an alley as Cope came out of the church.

Deborah levered the rifle and started after Cholla. Cope darted forward and cut her off.

"Stay out of this," he said as he reached her.

"This is my town," Deborah replied. "I'm in this."

"Then keep him pinned down till I get behind him."

Paying no heed, she continued her run toward the alley as Cope headed for the alley to the right. Entering, he kept up his trotting pace through the passageway, intending to circle Cholla.

Now aware of her mistake and her vulnerability, Deborah stopped at the entrance and hugged the front of the building, intending to survey the interior before entering. Unknown to her, Cholla had returned to the entrance, pressing himself against the side of the building. As Deborah leaned in for a look, Cholla grabbed the barrel of the rifle, yanking it, and her, into the passage. Thrown off balance, she stumbled, almost fell, and let go of the gun. Cholla heaved the Winchester into the street and pulled her to him, her back against his chest. His left arm went around her neck, putting pressure on her throat.

Cope appeared at the opposite end of the alley and, quickly assessing the scene before him, shouted, "Cholla!" as he advanced.

Cholla turned clumsily, maintaining his hold on Deborah. Hiding most of his body behind hers, Cholla created a stand-off. Cope stood his ground. He was not in control, but maybe he could turn the tables on Cholla.

"This ends now!"

"It ends when I say. Drop the gun or she die, just like your precious wife!"

To drive his point home, Cholla placed his revolver at Deborah's temple and cocked it. Though angered by Cholla's reference to E.J., Cope continued to think, fully aware of Cholla's capabilities. He stopped at ten yards away and assumed an acquiescent posture, letting the gun fall from his hand. As the weapon landed, Cholla quickly moved his revolver from Deborah and fired on Cope. The round entered Cope's chest just below the healed wound but slightly closer to center. Cope was doubled and shoved back several inches before being dumped on the ground on his back.

Reacting to this, Deborah squirmed and kicked her foot back into Cholla's shin, creating sharp pain. Cholla relaxed his grip on her. She fell away from him, lost footing and sprawled on the ground in front of him as Cholla turned his gun on her.

Forcing himself up on the elbow of his wounded arm, Cope took in the scene through clouding eyes. He'd kill her for sure. Through growing pain, he glanced to the Colt laying on the ground out of reach.

There was no chance of reaching it before Cholla fired.

Wait—the Derringer.

Ace in the hole.

His hand reached into his vest pocket and brought out the tiny Derringer which had rested in the garment, all but forgotten, since Cope's exit from Cimarron.

With Cholla's attention momentarily on Deborah, Cope cocked the little weapon and extended it. His fuzzy vision did not help. No time to waste and only two shots available. He pulled the trigger on the first barrel and the piece bucked in his hand, belching out a .44 slug. Cope watched and prepared to loose the second round, but Cholla buckled as the bullet sank into his belly. Cholla raised his pistol. Aim higher. Cope gritted his teeth, cocked the piece again and fired. Cholla's head kicked back sharply and his body pitched backward to the ground in a spread eagled position. He moved no more. Cope slipped down on his back but, remarkably, lucidity prevailed as the pain became debilitating.

Deborah watched Cholla fall, then moved her view to Cope as he dropped to his back.

"Worley!"

20

THE SCENE BEFORE DEBORAH AS SHE pulled herself up devastated her. First in her view was Cope on his back on the ground. Then she glanced again to her right to see Cholla, his body motionless, bullet holes in his gut and his forehead just above the right eye. Her immediate concern, Worley. He had proven himself correct regarding Cholla and now lay wounded for his attempt to save her life. She hauled herself up and rushed to his side, going to her knees and reaching her arm under his neck, lifting his head slightly. Still conscious but quite weak and obviously failing, Cope's eyes darted around and then settled on Deborah. Blood flowed from a corner of his mouth. Through labored, erratic breathing, he forced his voice to work.

"Cholla?"

"He's... dead."

Cope breathed a difficult sigh of relief. "Good."

Deborah stroked his forehead in a vain attempt to comfort him. "Don't talk. You're hurt bad."

"Don't matter now... Job's done ... over with."

Deborah leaned in closer. Way out here with no medical

help nearby, how could he survive? Still, she attempted to extend his life by comforting him. "Mr. Worley, please."

"Don't... fret yourself. Time's short... Need you... do something... for me."

"Yes, anything."

"My horse—bushes... behind church. Huey's money... in—in saddlebag... Find... letter there... addressed to... Rud Tanner. Post it for me... ."

"Of course, but, please, save your strength. Don't talk."

"No coming back... from this. Going home—home... to E.J."

"Your wife?" Her voice cracked with emotion.

Cope managed a weak smile. "Yeah. She's... waiting for me."

He turned his head to an image seen only by him. Deborah could only guess at what it was, but imagined E.J. standing there, her arms extended, waiting to embrace him. His face showed his anticipation.

"See? She's there... right there..." His hand reached for that which only he could see. "E.J., I'm here... ."

His body arched slightly in a futile attempt to get to her. Then his head fell limply to the side as his last breath escaped his lips.

Emotion encompassed Deborah. Tears filled her eyes as she gazed at Cope's limp form. She bowed her head and wept quietly, allowing tears to go unchecked as they coursed down her cheeks and dropped to comingle with the blood stains on his shirt.

Eiling arrived, limping, and managed to crouch. He sought a pulse. Deborah took in a deep, cleansing breath.

"My God, Mason," she managed in a shaky voice, "how he must have loved her. I only hope she was there for him when he passed. I hope they can be together forever."

Mason looked across at her. "They will."

They stayed there for several moments, weighing the enormity of the events and pondering the death of a close friend whom they never really knew. Then, ever so tenderly, Deborah placed Cope's head on the ground and got to her feet.

Tearing away the cloth of his trousers and examining Eiling's wound, she used a strip of her petticoat to bind it temporarily.

"It's all right," he said to reassure her, "It'll heal. Just hurts like the dickens."

"Stay here," she said, "I'll be back to help you."

Starting toward the church, she passed Cholla's body and tried in vain to keep from hating him. Her destination was the bushes behind the church to seek out Cope's horse and the contents of the saddle bag. Paying little attention to the package containing Huey's money, she searched for Cope's letter. As she pulled it free, she noticed the address. *Rud Tanner, c/o General Delivery, Senado Pass, Texas*, as well as the sparse return address, *Worley, Somewhere in Colorado*. Intrigued, she ventured a look inside and became immediately locked on the scribbled words therein.

They consumed her.

—

RUD TANNER SAT IN HIS FAVORITE position, legs propped on the tabletop with the chair rocked back on its rear legs. He pondered the two letters he had received this morning, one in each hand, debating which to open first. The discussion in his mind lived but a short time. He decided by the return addresses on the envelopes. One was from Cope and the other from a woman named Deborah Strawbridge at a place called God's Acre's. Utah Territory. Mighty strange name for a town. Still, he deemed the communication from Cope more important and proceeded to rip open its container. The note it revealed was brief.

Rud,

    If you are reading this, I am likely dead. What I cannot tell you is, if Cholla is dead as well. Right now, all I know is, I am close. It has been a long journey up to now and if I do not get Cholla it will be a waste. Please stop by E.J.'s grave, once in a while if you can, as, now, you are the only one left to care for it. You have been a good friend and I will miss you, but now I can be with E.J. again and always.

Your friend,
Cope

Tanner's face went white as a sudden chill took hold. Somewhere in the back of his mind, he had expected this news since the day Cope left on his hunt. But, to literally learn it from Cope himself, was, to say the least, unsettling. They'd agreed that they would likely never see each other again. This news would eventually come, but from a different source, a different way, surely not in Cope's own hand. Shaking his head in depression and clearing his throat of the impediment this had placed there, he lifted his legs and allowed the chair to come forward to its front supports, planting his feet tentatively on the floor.

"Shit!" That was all he could muster as he stared at the letter for a long, silent moment.

Reaching for the second communication, which had fallen into his lap as he changed position, curiosity briefly replaced his sense of loss. He inserted a finger in the flap and destroyed the envelope without effort. The letter inside encompassed several pages.

Dear Mr. Tanner,

    It is with a heavy heart that I must inform you of the death of your friend, Mr. Cope Worley. He died bravely, defending me and my town from the dangers posed by the man he identified to us as Lorenzo Cholla, who was passing himself off as a completely different person. I have forwarded, under separate cover, a letter that was penned by Mr. Worley prior to his arrival here and which I found in his effects after his unfortunate demise. I took the liberty of examining that document before sending it on to you. It is my fervent hope that it arrives in the company of my own letter since Mr. Worley's letter generated mine.

I have asked a bank to transfer the moneys found among Cholla's things as partial reparation for the funds Cholla stole from your bank.

I cannot adequately commend to you the courage Mr. Worley displayed, even to placing himself in a position of inevitable death, to save me and stop Cholla. While I may not agree with his tactics, I completely understand his motives and his desire to see the murderer of his beloved wife brought to justice. This he has done. I can only hope that I, someday, am the recipient of a love such as must have existed between Mr. Worley and his late wife.

Please be assured we have held a proper funeral for Mr. Worley and interred him in a place marked with honor befitting his ultimate sacrifice. Although they are not buried together, I am certain that he and his wife are together again in Heaven and will remain so for all time.

Please join me in praying for the soul of this gallant man who will remain in our thoughts for many years to come.

Your Obedient Servant,
Deborah Strawbridge

Now, thoroughly shaken, Tanner wiped an errant tear from his eye as this hit him full on. Cope was gone. He ain't no more.

Usually not one to succumb to emotion, the pain of loss exceeding what he experienced at E.J.'s death returned to overwhelm him. This moved him to go to her grave then and there. Not to tend to it, as Cope had requested. He would do that, of course, in time, but now, he would talk to E.J. She might already know all this, but still, he had to tell her, to read these words to her. She had to know.

BOB GIEL WAS BORN IN NEW YORK City and now lives in New Jersey. He has been in love with the Western genre since he was a kid, and absorbed so much of the period through books, movies, and television that he feels as though he could easily have been there himself. The grit and the determination of the people who carved a way of life out of the frontier have helped shape the way Bob lives his life. Because of that era, he keeps his word, he finishes what he starts, and he is a true friend. While he was always interested in writing, life got in the way, that is, until he retired. With the decks cleared, he began writing and never looked back.